Quick Walk to Murder

jd daniels

QUICK WALK to MURDER

THE SECOND JESSIE MURPHY MYSTERY

jd daniels

SAVVY PRESS
NEW YORK

ISBN: 978-1508823070

Library of Congress Cataloging-in-Publication Data: 201590430
Quick Walk to Murder: a novel/jd daniels—1st ed.
1. Matlacha (Florida)—Mystery. 2. Women artists
Fiction. 3. Crab Fishing (Florida) Fiction.

Jacket artist: Peg Cullen
Cover design by Carrie Spencer

Printed in the United States of America
SAVVY PRESS – GAWANUS BOOKS – SAGE SF PUBLISHERS
Distributed Worldwide
FIRST EDITION

Very few of us are what we seem.
~ Agatha Christie

For my loved ones . . . always

1

The shadowy form of a four-foot snook shot through the waters like a torpedo and disappeared under the dark depths of the dock. Vehicles roared across the drawbridge. A kayaker in the mist lifted her black paddle and making a flapping wing motion, waved. I raised my free hand in greeting, gripping my packed bag. A great blue heron strolled toward two cormorants preening on a decayed piling. The splintered railing felt rough, raw—capable of giving pain. It was late April and past time to leave Matlacha (say Mat-la`-shay) and return once again . . . alone . . . to Cambridge.

When I first ventured to the islands with Will in my innocent, love-struck early twenties, Matlacha seemed the most magical, perfect place in the world. That everything was goodness and light. That nothing dark, and certainly not evil, happened. Last year, when I returned and found out Will had been murdered, I was forced to face that I'd been wrong.

My plan as I drove back north was to take a good calculated look at myself. Something had to change. Here was what I knew: Name? Jessie Murphy. Stats? Twenty-eight. Single. Paid my bills by managing a few apartments in Cambridge, Massachusetts. Saved enough in six months to travel to a funky, artsy fishing village where I painted and showed my work in the local galleries. Life was good. More than good. But the biological clock was ticking. I wanted a family. Yet, and this was a BIG yet . . . I couldn't make the move to do anything about it.

Chicken. Pure spicy freckled chicken. That was me.

Footsteps pounded. I turned and smiled at my always-good-for-a-laugh friend, Zen. Her thick, now shoulder-length black hair looked like she'd not taken time to comb it. With the extra thirty pounds she carried, it wasn't surprising that she was out of breath. Seeing her red and swollen eyes, I loosened my grip on the handle of the bag. "What's wrong?" I asked, looking down at her.

I was five-eight. She was five-two. We were within a couple of years of being the same age. My face was freckled. Hers was flawless and baby doll round.

Zen burst into tears. "Oh, Jessie! Tomas is dead! Gator said he was murdered."

Blood rushed from my face. "Tomas? Tomas is dead?"

She nodded.

I dropped the bag, hurried to her side, took her elbow and led her to an Adirondack chair.

"Oh, Jessie!" The howl that came from Zen sent the cormorants skyward. I reached for her interlocked fingers.

"When?"

Zen's body shuddered. She blinked and then spoke in a husky voice. "Gator found him last night. He hadn't come to Bert's in a couple of days and we'd begun to wonder what happened to him. It wasn't like Tomas not to stop by for a chat after his tours. Gator found him lying in his own, oh . . . on the floor . . . in the bathroom." Her phrases sounded like they were buzzed in two by a saw blade.

I worked hard at not letting the picture focus vividly in my head. If the images got too clear, I knew I'd have nightmares. I'd have to spend the next weeks and months painting them away and I really, really wanted to paint positive images: Like Canada geese heading south in synchronized flight and pelicans swimming a perfect Vformation in calm waters, or tourists sunning under umbrellas while little urchins played with their yellow and red buckets as fishermen pulled in grouper. Images that would assure me I was okay. Because I was okay. I was.

Zen's clutch could snap one of my brushes in two.

I would stay for the funeral, of course.

Since my efficiency was already rented and all other rooms were booked at the island motels and inns, Zen offered to have me stay with her and her current boyfriend, Zebra. Zen said he got his handle at the Naples Zoo where he had befriended one. I wondered if it had more to do with the bleached stripes in his dyed black hair. But they only had a one-bedroom trailer and I had seen the couch. Well, I thought what I'd seen was a couch. So I opted to call around for a motel room for three nights. That, I assumed, would be all that I would need to attend the service, comfort Zen and Gator, then be on my way.

Jake, the baby boomer who filled in for me as manager of two apartment complexes in Cambridge, was heading for Costa Rica in a couple of days. It turned out Jake's current companion was not a flexible person. She wanted him on the flight beside her. If Jake missed the flight, so be it, I'd assured him. The foxy college freshman could go on without him. Since he was almost sixty and had spent painstakingly precious minutes of his time picking out and purchasing her string bikini and yellow bamboo nightie and thong, he wasn't keen on someone else having the first peek at her in them. So he insisted I needed to get back. Of course I did.

The only place with a room was a cheap motel in North Fort Myers. I preferred island life on Matlacha, but had no choice. I put Gar, my plaster of Paris yard art gargoyle and companion, on the counter, ignoring the sideway looks of the guy who checked me in. He was unshaven and his yellow-toothed grin was more sneer than smile. His eyes never left my T-shirt. It took all of the discipline I had not to escape the room, run to my car and return to the fishing village where one-story cottages and duplexes stood next to three-story

3

million-dollar homes. Where yachts harbored in the same bay as one-person flat-bottom skiffs that looked like they'd sink at the next crab-trap check. With great effort I managed to overpower my urge to leave. Be brave, I told myself.

Minutes later Zen arrived. "Come on, let's get out of here. I found a tent. You can sleep in the backyard."

I looked at the clouds and mouthed "Thank you."

2

Gator, a local who like Zen, had helped me in my investigation last season, stood three feet from the canal holding a crab trap. His skin was tanned a deep shade of brown. His arms and legs were thin, wiry and dotted by age spots. His pocked, bulbous nose came to a severe point at the tip. Every move was slow and seemed to have purpose. Unhooking the latch, he turned the trap over and two crabs dropped to the ground and quick-walked sideways to the edge of the seawall. Then, splat. Splat. They were gone.

"Like to trap them, but can't stand to kill them. Don't know why, don't have the same issue with fish. Tomas had the same problem when he was a kid, but he soon learned they were his folks' bread and butter and got over it." Gator had on a black T-shirt and cut-offs. The shirt was adorned with a colorful crab. "Crab Love" was imprinted under the crustacean. If I wasn't still in shock over the news of Tomas's murder, I would have smiled. Gator's bushy beard needed trimming. He had a gold earring in his left ear. His expression was solemn. He nodded and went to the clay firepot and stoked it. Leave it to Zen to have a burning pot in her backyard that looked like it belonged in front of a Buddhist temple.

I set down my bag. "It's horrible about Tomas."

"Yeah!" Gator spat into a flowering, poisonous oleander. Zen gushed out of the trailer with two bottles of beer and handed one to me.

Gator scowled, tossing back a gulp of Bud. Mumbling, he drew the back of his hand across his lips. "I could drown myself. It makes me so blasted mad." His voice caught.

Zen came to his side. Her arm encircled his shoulder. I collapsed into a lawn chair.

"Tomas's mom is Mexican. You think it was a hate crime?" Zen asked.

Gator sniffed loudly and spat into the plant again. "Could be. Tomas came to me and said he was in trouble. Said he was afraid for his life. But no matter how often I asked, he wouldn't tell me who was after him or what had happened." Gator reached under his chair and pulled out a bulging manila envelope wrapped in cellophane. "He said if anything happened to him, I was to give you this. I promised him I wouldn't snoop and I didn't either. He said for you to open it in private."

I was incredulous. "But why me? I hardly knew him? I only met him a couple of times. I mean, he was a nice guy and all, but I didn't know him! There was no way I could have meant anything to Tomas. I'm just one of many artists who paints in the area. I'm not even a permanent resident. What could I possibly have been to him?"

"Don't know, girl. I only know what happened. Here, take it!" He dropped the package in my lap as if it was a hot rock.

"Everyone knows how you solved Will and Rose's deaths," Zen said. "Tomas didn't have to know you personally to realize what you are capable of, hon."

Great. Just great.

"But I'll have to go to the cops and tell them about this," I said.

Gator nodded. "Yeah. Yeah. Yeah. I figure you'll have to turn it over, but first you got to see it. Right? I mean, those are a dead man's wishes."

6

I let out a heavy sigh. I'd do my duty and open the envelope, but tomorrow morning I'd make the call. I wanted this thing off my plate. I needed to get back to my job. I stood. "Guess I'll take a walk."

Zen held up her beer. "I'll get your tent ready. Sure hope it doesn't leak."

I pretended I hadn't heard her as I rounded the trailer and walked down May Street. Luckily it was a full moon. A man on a bicycle rode toward me. Tucking the envelope under my arm, I quickened my step and headed toward the community park where I would open the package on my favorite bench facing the Matlacha Pass. There was nothing more soothing than listening to the lapping of the water on the shore. And I needed some SERIOUS soothing time.

"Ouch!" I swatted my neck as I stepped into a swarm of worse-than-mosquitoes-no-see-ums. The package was rubbing my underarm raw. I removed it, but refused to look at it. What you can't see isn't there, right? I smacked my forearm. "Dammit."

Jogging across the two-lane county road, I veered right, then left, heading for the park. Hesitating, I watched a gopher tortoise. Thick neck extended, nose high. Regal as it lumbered into low-lying grasses. Was the prehistoric looking beast telling me to slow down? Perhaps. Just perhaps. Nature has plenty of messages for us, Grandma Murphy always said. I lowered my arms and continued on at a slower pace.

Should have been through southern Florida by now, dreaming about being tucked into a pillow, watching CSI or Criminal Minds, my TV comfort food. Instead, I was heading toward a place I'd thought I'd already given my farewell.

I put my hand on the natural rock sculpture that stood beside the bench. "You didn't expect me, did you Odessa?" I am one of those people who named inanimate objects and then talked to them as if they were human. Like Gar, for instance. He was sitting on the front seat of my car, securely strapped in, waiting patiently for me to climb in behind the steering wheel. Right now, I was wishing he were with me.

7

Sitting, I shook the curious envelope. It rattled. Tearing off the plastic, ripping the envelope open, I pulled out a package wrapped in white paper imprinted with a badly drawn design of an owl. I unwrapped that and grimaced.

With distaste, I picked up a ten-inch plastic skeleton dressed as a woman in a faded rose-colored dress and a tattered hat. Inspecting it, I recalled the time Grandma Murphy had scared me half to death one Halloween night when I was a toddler by dangling a super large skeleton from the limb of a tree. It had taken me several years before I would let Mom take me to Grandma's to Trick or Treat.

Why had Tomas instructed Gator to give this to me? And why no note of explanation? Why couldn't he just spit out the meaning?

Puzzled, and more than irritated, I rewrapped it and trekked slowly back to Zen's through the community park. Telling her and Gator I was exhausted and assuring them (to their more than curious dismay) I would reveal the contents of the package in the morning, I looked into the tent. Zen had the edge of the sleeping bag pulled back. She had taken Gar from my car and put him in the tent. I stepped in, zipped up the door, slipped out of my clothes, and slid into the bag. With my hand on Gar's ear, I gazed out the screened window.

The stars were as plentiful as daisies in my beloved Grandma Murphy's garden. The moon was a narrow crescent. A male laughed. A dog pushed around a bucket on a cement surface. The tent smelled of must, of sweat and of sex. I mean, Zen, REALLY? A door slammed. I closed my peepers and Tomas's face materialized. My eyes popped open. I sat up, grabbed Gar and slid him into the sleeping bag. Holding him close, I pressed my eyelids shut.

3

"Goodness, girl, look at your face! You've been eaten like an ear of corn on the cob!" Zen said. "Didn't you use that mosquito repellent I put in there?"

Flipping the sleeping bag off my aching body, I moaned. I felt like I'd been nibbled on by piranhas. I glanced around. The spray bottle stuck out from under the sleeping bag. I sniffed and raked my arms with the back of my hand.

"I was always told that going into nature soothed the soul. Guess that's another of those untrue myths." Zen winked and dropped the flap.

Pushing myself up from the hard surface, I warned myself to stop scratching. But that was like asking me not to sketch or paint. I cut a glance to the corner. The package had fallen over in the night near Gar's feet. I dressed and then grabbed it, leaving Gar. By the time I reached the kitchen, my flesh was raw and bright pink.

"Hey! I can't even look at you. Run some water over that face and those arms and legs." Zen rushed from the room.

I went to the sink, set the package on the counter, turned on the faucet, and did what I was told. But the scalding water wasn't hot enough. I pressed my lips together.

Zen appeared at my side and handed me an opened bottle of rubbing alcohol. "This will sting, but it'll take away the itch. Use these cotton balls."

It stung all right. Real sting. The kind of sting that makes your nose hairs twitch and your eyes fill with tears. I avoided looking at the package. Was it some kind of voodoo doll emitting a no-see-um-go-get-her curse?

"Ah, come on, it's not that bad." Zen handed me a cup of coffee strong enough to take my attention off my violated skin, but not off the skeleton doll. "Aren't you going to show me what's it?"

I had refused to let Gator or Zen see it last night, believing the thing would seem less menacing in the morning light. It would. I was sure of it. I nudged it toward her.

Zen tore at the paper and exploded in laughter. Then probably remembering that Tomas had left it as a clue to his murder, sobered. "I'm sorry, but look at it. It's like some Halloween toy for a kid." She turned it this way and that. "I've seen these skeletons in Halloween shops. Nice hat, huh?"

Of course it was laughable. It hadn't scared me. Not one bit.

"Why do you think Tomas wanted you to see this?"

"I'd hoped you might know."

"Nah, no way. But, hey, maybe Gator will."

I took three swallows and emptied the cup. Eww. "Good coffee."

"Yeah, it's instant, but I like it better after it's brewed in my coffee pot."

I resisted the urge to raise my eyebrows. Brewed instant coffee? Uh, huh. I shot a look at her pot. Like when had it ever been cleaned? Like NEVER! I set down my mug.

Leaving the macabre doll on the counter, I suggested we eat at the local breakfast and lunch spot, The Perfect Cup, where I figured news would be darting around faster than a hummingbird. It was also Gator's usual morning hangout. Even though accommodations were impossible to find, the majority of tourists and snowbirds had left. Traffic was cut in half. The shops were quieter. When we arrived the popular café actually had a few empty chairs and was occupied mostly by locals. Three weeks ago it would have been a different story.

We took a seat near the window and Pete at the next table included us in a conversation that appeared to have been going on for some time.

Pete was a ringer for Clint Eastwood. "The kid was depressed about a breakup with his girl. She's the daughter of some wealthy Sarasota businessman Tomas met at college. After meeting his parents—Shorty, we all know, is a local crabber, Mariana's from Mexico—without an explanation, she dumped him. What a crock of grouper guts."

Pete's fishing buddy, Bill, one of the well-known all-around nice guys, added his six cents' worth. "We've never seen the girl, but we want nothing to do with her. She obviously thinks she puts her britches on different than us."

"She'd just better not show her face at the funeral," Pete added.

Resting my arms on the table, I sipped my orange juice. Zen stood and went to the coffee counter and began speaking to Jay Mann, a local sculptor who had been trying for months (like since I'd arrived in November) to start a relationship with me. Zen's head lowered. Jay patted her shoulder and turned, walking directly my way.

"Tragic news, huh?" I said.

He pulled up a metal chair. His completely bald head, which I suspected he shaved, glistened. "Disgusting. Such a waste of a fine brain and young man." Jay's chest hair curled around the edge of his V-neck shirt.

I looked to the right of his ear, not into his blue eyes. "Yeah."

Jay cleared his throat. "See it?"

I frowned. "What?"

"Look closer. You aren't paying attention to the details. Look beyond the words." His sentences came out in a soft, evocative whisper. I leaned forward on my arms and took in the room. People were talking to anyone who would listen. I tuned out the words and focused on their faces, their body

11

language. And I glimpsed it. Angst. Barely hidden nervousness. Fear. I blinked rapidly and turned toward Jay. "What are they afraid of?"

"The truth," Jay said, gazing steadily into my guarded eyes. "Zen is sure she can raise enough money to pay you if you'll stay and investigate. She doesn't trust the cops. They're too willing to believe the worst of locals, especially those with immigrant blood."

Great. Just great. Stay in no-see-um purgatory while spring flowers blossomed around my northern apartment. Just what I wanted. Jay gave one quick nod and Zen hurried to the table. Sitting, she reached over and took my hand. My thin digits disappeared under her fleshy fingers. Although I was taller, Zen was a more robust woman. It was like she was the mother manatee and I was her calf. I liked Zen from the first time I met her. I also had an affinity for manatees. Every once in a while, I wondered if the two attractions had a cosmic connection.

"Oh, hon, thanks for doing this. I just know you can get to the bottom of his murder. His folks don't have much money, but we'll have a couple of fundraisers. Don't you worry, you'll get paid for your time."

Jay leaned toward the center of the table. Zen and I did the same. "But promise us you'll be careful. Their fear is a very real emotion and it takes a lot of evil to make fisher folks that scared."

I thought of the female skeleton Tomas Moore had left for me—a symbol of death—but why female? Was this a warning of what would happen if I got involved?

Zen squeezed my hand. I had to be honest with them.

"I'm not a Private Eye, you know. I'm a peon. I was a secretary in a detective office—not a detective." I did have my AA in criminology, but I'd never held a job where I officially used it, just dogged around after my boss on a few cases. Of course, there was what happened last year, me solving Will's murder. And, yes. Zen knew about this. So did everyone.

"We don't care nothin' about credentials," Zen said. "It's results that impress us."

I turned my cap to the side of my head. "Listen, I'm not the best person. Please talk to the Moores about hiring someone else. There are plenty of highly qualified people in the area."

Jay looked at his watch, excused himself and hurried out the door as Gator walked in. Seeing him, Zen and I turned him around and took him back to her trailer. He looked at the skeleton and shrugged. "That's one odd sight," he said. "Must have something to do with his background."

"Tomas ever show you anything like this before?"

"Nah," Gator said.

I looked at Zen. "You?"

"Nope."

"Got any ideas?"

They both shrugged and shook their heads.

I had to admit, I was with them. My brain cells were sleeping.

"You going to help find his killer?" Gator asked.

"I really don't know. Someone else…"

"Ah, give it up, girl. We need ya. You may not be much, but you're the best we got."

Like, THANK YOU very much!

Appearing assured I would take the case, Zen headed for her job. Gator made a beeline for his boat.

"But Gator, you said . . ."

"Tarpon's in. The cops know where to find me."

"But, Gator . . ."

"You heard me. Tarpon's in."

Putting the doll on my sleeping bag, I took several photos, then decided it was time for a quick power walk. Walking was my best thinking time. I changed into tennis shoes and walking shorts. Pulling on my cap, I trotted across Island Avenue. I'd been here for five and a half months with no demands for my PI skills. I had hoped to leave that way. My easel, sketchpad, and paints were all securely packed into the trunk of my car. The gas tank was full and the oil had been changed.

A great blue heron moved toward me, head high. I was always surprised how tame the birds often were. I stopped. One more step and I could bend and touch it. But the bird wasn't having any. It spread its wings and shot across the narrow canal. Cooling down, thinking of Tomas, I retraced my steps.

The tourist village consisted of a conglomeration of pastel and brightly painted galleries, gift shops, restaurants, inns and motels, bait shops, and canal-lined homes built on landfill. Shack-sized buildings, mobile homes, modest one-story houses and million-dollar mansions were constructed beside each other. Boats were moored behind most buildings. When the area was first settled, it had been dubbed Matlacha, possibly a name meaning "water to the chin" given by the original inhabitants, the Calusa Indians. With four hundred plus residences, a busy narrow street and a drawbridge that cut the town in two, it was a place easy to pass through.

I walked to the edge of the canal and hopped onto a rusty almost blue metal boat used for who knew what. Hunkering down, I placed my fingers in the water and wiggled them. A manatee stretched her snout toward my hand. Her expression wasn't unlike the look a mother gives her infant, warm and loving.

Goose bumps rose on my flesh. This was why I had returned to this island—why after swearing off Florida, I had reversed my decision in November. Some said I'd done it because I hated winter, others insisted it was to feel close to the ghost of Will, but the solid truth had to do with these animals and the creative, magical energy that permeated the place. These two things signified something primeval and imaginative, but guileless, forthright, and self-assured. When I took a walk I stood up taller, lengthened my stride; gave a nod to the clouds. The energy was God-like. Some didn't feel this or get it. But the people I talked to did and no one could do justice in trying to describe it.

The manatee swam away. I stood.

One of the owners of C W Fudge, Chris Efron, a cross between Andrew Garfield, the current Spider Man and actor Johnny Depp, stood chatting with a man at the rear of the shop. According to Zen, the customers who visited the store were not there just for the candy. Just looking at and talking with Chris kept them smiling for the rest of the day. Word had it that he had quit his career in corporate America to follow his dream of owning a candy store. Whenever he dated a local woman, the Perfect Cup and the Mermaid Spa buzzed for weeks. Chris and his business partner made and sold the best chocolate and peanut butter fudge made out of real cream and butter that I'd ever eaten. Sorry, Grandma. Not that yours wasn't good. And his chocolate turtles and various other candy animals and birds? To kill for.

I slowed my pace and dropped my arms to my side. The man who had been talking to Chris tipped his cap at me as he passed.

"Hey, Chris, bad news, huh?"

"The worst. You staying for the funeral?"

"Yeah." Releasing my cell phone from its waist clip, I pushed down on the camera icon. "You ever seen anything like this?"

Chris gazed at the photo of the skeleton doll, blinked several times and diverted his eyes. "Sure, in New Orleans at Mardi Gras. You see them in all the windows."

I looked at the image, the doll's floppy hat, then at Chris. Was I wrong or was he all of a sudden nervous?

"Ever seen one around here?"

An osprey landed in a nest on a telephone pole. A brown pelican waddled along the gravel near a parked car. Chris cleared his throat. "Nah, not that I know of."

I kept my voice casual. "How well did you know Tomas?"

"Not well. Bought any owl-shaped candy we made for his mom when he was home. He didn't talk much. Ran in and out

15

fast. Always seemed to be in a hurry." The front door to the shop opened. "Got to go. See you there." He nodded and left.

The osprey raised its wings and dove toward the canal. When it soared high, a mullet dangled from its talons. The talons opened and the dying fish fell, defiling my tennis shoes. I tugged on the bill of my cap.

A black eye stared up at me. A fin quivered.

I shuddered.

4

I knew where the County Sheriff's office was in Fort Myers, but I had never met his replacement. That I was the cause of the past sheriff being imprisoned as an accomplice in a murder was on my mind as I pulled into the parking lot. The present sheriff and his deputies would know who I was, of course. Word got around fast. Faces were known. I wouldn't be shocked if I found mine pasted on a bulletin board here being used as a target for darts.

It didn't surprise me to see the same dispatcher at the reception desk. That she wasn't very friendly didn't astonish me either.

"Is the sheriff in?"

"Yes."

"I'd like to see him."

"*He* is a *she* and she is busy." The woman concentrated on her computer screen.

My grin was thin as I swallowed my PC mistake. "That's okay. I can wait." I sauntered away with my tail between my long, willowy legs. The woman's fingers continued to tap the keyboard. A clear glass vase was filled with several white gardenia blossoms. I leaned forward to smell them. The door to the back offices opened, a man in a business suit came out and walked toward the entrance.

Another woman in a tan uniform stood in the doorway with her hand on the jamb. Her hair was auburn and pulled back into a bun. She was about five-nine and slender. Turquoise-framed glasses made her look more like an academic than an officer of the law. It had to be the sheriff. She nodded at me and began to release the door. It was obvious the dispatcher had no intention of introducing us.

"Excuse me!" In a rush of words, I asked if I could have a moment of her time. After a brief hesitation, she nodded, stepped back and walked along the hallway. I tossed the dispatcher a triumphant look, and hurried into the corridor, following her into a room I'd never been in before. Apparently Sheriff White (her name was on a plaque on her desk) preferred fresh digs. The previous office had been across the hall.

"Thanks so much for seeing me." I took the chair facing her.

"You caught me at a good time. The last meeting was shorter than I planned." Her eyes were blue and didn't waver from mine. "Well?"

I reached into my handbag and handed over the package, explaining how I came by it. She opened it, took out the skeleton and set it on her desk. "These people are so religious, aren't they?"

These people??

I shifted uncomfortably in my chair.

"Doesn't this have to do with the Day of the Dead—one of those Mexican holidays—something about honoring and celebrating the dead or whatever? I think they have wild parades and wear costumes. Very quaint."

The woman's scorn was way too obvious. I wasn't impressed.

"Perhaps."

"Why do you think Tomas Moore left this for you?"

"I really don't know, but I thought you should have it."

"And who gave it to you?"

I gave her Gator's name.

"Real name?"

Good question. No idea.

She ran her tongue around the inside of her mouth. "You were a friend of the deceased?"

"Not that close. I met him a couple of times."

"Most murder victims are killed by a friend or a family member. You know that, right?"

I frowned and nodded. Was she trying to intimidate me? If so, why?

She looked at my hair, then seemed to be taking in my freckles. "Irish?"

I smiled.

"Perhaps he thought you'd understand the superstitious implications. The Irish believe in elves and such things, don't they?"

I was taken aback. Where did they get THESE people? "Some do, some don't."

She hesitated, then said, "Thank you, Ms. Murphy, for bringing this in. Our investigation is ongoing. We want this case put to rest more than anyone. Please leave your name and contact information at the front desk."

I headed for the door.

"Oh, and Ms. Murphy,"

I turned around.

"I suggest you advise the parents to let us do our job and to stay out of our business. Independent people like crabbers tend to want to take care of their own problems, but hopefully, this won't be the situation here. We don't need non-professionals mucking up our case." A small smile curled her lips, but her gaze was lined in slivers of steel. "And, again, give them our condolences."

Was that a warning to stay out of it? I tugged down on the bill of my cap and lowered my head, kind of like a bull shark getting ready to strike. Luckily I was able to control my voice. "I'll be sure to give them your message."

She shuffled papers on her desk, but didn't look up. "You were the one who helped solve the Rolins case last year, right?"

So she had recognized my name. "Yeah."

She glanced at the clock. "Goodbye, Ms. Murphy. Have a safe trip home."

As I walked down the hall, a deputy came toward me. I looked away. He brushed my shoulder as he passed.

"Excuse me," he said in a friendly voice.

I kept walking.

Issuing a warning to a Murphy to stay away was like refusing to share a plate of soft peanut butter fudge, something, even if on a strict diet, the Murphys could never resist taking. And so I would stay. I would investigate. I would search for the truth that many apparently found so fearful to face. And I would buy some Skin So Soft (the best mosquito repellent made) from the woman who sold Avon at the post office and buy two, no three bottles of rubbing alcohol. And I'd prove once again that artists, and Irish women, are not irrational fools.

Sliding in behind the steering wheel, I phoned Zen. "I'm in," I said.

The next place to go was to the parents, the Moores, but I wouldn't do that yet. Not until after the funeral. People deserved private family time to mourn. Instead, I headed my car north. Sarasota was less than two hours away. Zen had given me the name of the ex-girlfriend. It hadn't been difficult to find out her parents' name and address—even the phone number. Switchboard.com was such a handy internet tool. But I wouldn't phone ahead. I preferred to not give people a chance to consider their story.

My phone's GPS led me right to their doorstep. I wondered if the girlfriend would be present. In fact, would anyone be home? That was the downside of wanting the element of surprise—I might find only disappointment.

The cream stucco house was fronted with a long staircase tapering from spacious to narrow as it reached the double doors. Two potted palm trees flanked the peach-colored doors. Lifting the knocker, I tapped brass against brass several times and then stood back to wait. The door opened and a uniformed Latino woman with a stern expression faced me. After giving my name, the maid left, then returned within a minute.

"They are very tired, but agreed to see you briefly." Exuding winter frost, she stepped back. I followed her down a wide hallway, through a high-ceilinged living room, to a screened enclosure that in Florida was called a lanai. The pool was kidney-shaped. A man and a woman sat at a wrought iron table. A blonde younger woman in a bikini was stretched out on a lounge chair. The maid introduced me and left. I was encouraged to sit and noted that the young woman had not looked up from her magazine when I was introduced. In fact, if anything, she had buried her head deeper into the pages.

The woman (Mrs. Howard?) offered lemonade. I accepted.

The man, whose bushy unkempt white hair reminded me of Einstein or Mark Twain, folded his hands on a table cluttered with what looked like mail. "I'm afraid I'm at a disadvantage. Mia said your name is Ms. Murphy. I don't believe we've met."

"No, we haven't had the pleasure of meeting. I, uh, hope you don't mind. I've come at a sad time."

Mrs. Howard twisted toward her husband. "A sad time? Is it our son? Has something happened to Robert?" Her face paled to a faded pink shade.

"Oh, no, not at all," I said. "You haven't heard?"

"Haven't heard what?" Mr. Howard reached for his wife's hand.

I glanced toward the blonde. The magazine was on her lap. Her eyes were wide.

As if to shelter myself from being the one to give the news, I raised my hands. "I am so sorry to be the one to tell you this. I assumed you'd heard. Tomas Moore is dead. I believe you knew him."

Mr. and Mrs. Howard rose as one and rushed toward their daughter. "Oh, Caitlin!"

The girl's gasp and moan was muffled in the mother's robe.

I felt like an ogre. Why did I have to be the one to give the news? I rubbed my forehead and slid back from the table. Mrs. Howard helped her daughter stand, and holding her upright assisted her out of the screened room. Mr. Howard returned to the table.

"I should leave." I pushed up from the chair. I hated situations like this more than I hated raw fish.

"No. Please. Sit." He retook his chair.

"I'm so sorry, I assumed you'd know. I really should go."

His shoulders slumped. "I'm sure we would have been informed sooner, but we've been abroad. We just returned. We weren't to be back until tonight, but I got a touch of dysentery, so we returned earlier than expected. I needed a vacation, so I asked for none of my messages to be forwarded. I even was able to talk Caitlin and my wife into leaving their cell phones home. Let me tell you that that took some doing. No one feels safe anymore unless they're carrying a cell phone. Oddly enough, Caitlin hasn't been able to find her phone since we got back. How absolutely dreadful. That poor boy. Oh, dear, poor Caitlin."

The cement pelican that stood at the edge of the pool seemed so stoic, so totally untouched by emotion—a blessing. I had to continue. That was my job. I sat. "I'm a friend of the family. They're devastated, of course."

"Tomas was like a son. How tragic." Mr. Howard hung his head. "How terrible—dead—Oh . . ." He raised his moistened eyes. "How did he die?"

"He was murdered."

Mr. Howard straightened in his chair. "Not possible!" His voice was a bomb in the quiet room. The ice in the lemonade glasses shook. "I just can't believe . . ."

Minutes later, after Mrs. Howard, looking paler and even more distraught, reentered the room and comforted her husband, I excused myself. I would come back another time.

With my hand on the doorknob, I felt as if I were being watched. I turned. In a far doorway I spied the disappearing leg of dark trousers. My eyes searched higher. Caitlin Howard stood at the top of the staircase that overlooked the living room and front door. In the split second after our eyes met, the girl walked slowly away.

Where had the rumor begun that the parents were against this relationship? Certainly not with the father or mother. Unless the man was lying and my instincts said he wasn't. Who was the person who had obviously been listening to the conversation but had not shown themselves? The son? Another employee? Someone who didn't want to be seen, that was obvious.

As I drove away I began to compose a list: The girl's parents. The girl. Her brother. Tomas's family. Those Tomas worked for at the kayak tour company. Perhaps a roommate at college. Close friends. Professors who knew him. I was sure there were others, but this would be a beginning. Possible motives had yet to be uncovered.

There always had to be a place to start.

5

Knowing Tomas's family were crabbers, I decided to visit the Pine Island Library to use one of their computers. One of these days I should buy a laptop to use when away from Cambridge, but this computer access was handy enough.

There was minimal information about two of the fish companies, but the St. James City one was launched in 1990. I wanted to know who the owners were, but no owner or phone number was listed. That meant I'd have to go to the place. No problem. It was a simple, ten-minute drive down a two-lane highway I'd taken many times. One of my favorite restaurants was at the tip of St. James. I'd spent many a day sketching at one of the outside tables facing the Gulf.

I clicked off that site and typed in "Day of the Dead." The sheriff was right. In Mexican culture costumed female skeletons were used to help honor the dead. But this made no sense. Why leave me such a thing? And why say for it not to be opened unless something happened to him?

Leaving the building, I skipped down the steps with the idea of visiting the fish house, but froze in mid-step. What if people there knew Tomas and hadn't heard about his murder? He was a local who had been raised, played ball, gone to school, and to church in Pine Island. Could I face another scene like what happened at the Howards? Absolutely not. I would hold my investigative work until after the funeral. Surely by then people would have read *The Eagle* or have heard by word of mouth about the young man. I did not want to be the one to give the news again. Call me a chicken, but I'd wait.

If I kept my eyes open, there might be someone at the funeral who I could add to my list. More than one killer not able to help themselves showed up at a funeral of their victim.

A room opened up at the Bridgewater Inn in Matlacha and I phoned Zen and told her I would no longer need the tent in her backyard. I was fortunate to catch the postmistress and even more fortunate that she happened to have a full supply of Avon goodies in the trunk of her car. I bought her largest bottle of Skin So Soft.

At the inn I removed Gar from the front seat and unpacked. Since my boyfriend Will Rolins` murder, Gar who I'd rescued from a garbage can, served as my sole confidant and my travel companion. I knew this was pathetic, but I just wasn't ready to invite a human into my inner life just yet. Of course I relied on my beloved Grandma Murphy's wisdom as well, but I couldn't haul her around with me. She used a walker now and didn't leave her home much. Gar had had this role before Will's death, but now he was even more important to my sense of well-being. He was the one possession I wouldn't sell for a million bucks.

After generously applying the repellent, I sat out on the dock to sketch in pastels, knowing I had a comfortable, no-see-um-free bed waiting. A mechanical crane dropped repeatedly onto a bridge piling, sinking an upright post deep into the sandy floor. I focused on a scene and the loud construction site noise drifted into oblivion.

The horizon shimmered in vivid orange and pale yellow, pink and indigo. Dusty blue tails divided orange hues. Palm fronds swayed. The pass rippled in shades of ochre and purple. A brilliant red flame backlit one sable palm as the sun set and my cheeks felt the gentleness of the evening breeze. I was in

Matlacha, a funky, magical place where my dreams almost always outwitted my nightmares.

The echo of footfalls on the dock made my head turn. It was Zen, and again she wasn't smiling her usual cheerful smile. "Hey, you busy?" she asked, flopping down on a striped blue and yellow fish-shaped Adirondack chair.

"What do you think?"

"Okay, stupid question. You're working. How's this? Are you ready to take a break yet? Bert's is calling."

"Let me put this away," I said as I gathered up my pastels and pad.

"Can I see it?"

Zen knew by now that you never, never looked at an artist's work without permission. Many knew it, the difference was, Zen honored the concept. Because of this, I was always ready for her to take a look. I turned the pastel drawing pad toward her.

She leaned forward gazing at the 11x14 drawing. "You got it right, girl. I was just looking at that sunset myself. It was a kicker, that one."

Nodding my thanks, I stood. Zen opened the door, but remained on the dock. I placed the painting near Gar and patted his head.

When I stepped outside Zen interlocked her arm in mine. "I know you didn't know Tomas like me and Gator did and I just want you to know that we appreciate what you're doing."

"I'll do my best." We took a right toward Bert's. "Tell me what you knew about him."

"Tomas? He was real smart. That's how he got to go to college. Got a scholarship. The lucky sti . . . I mean guy, well, I guess I don't mean that at all. Guess he wasn't so lucky after all."

"Did he ever help his folks in the crabbing business?"

"Sure, 'til he was about sixteen, I guess. When he turned sixteen his mama said she didn't want him to do it no more. Said he should spend his time studyin`. If you ask me, he was glad to quit."

"Did he date much in high school? Carouse?"

"Nah, he always said he didn't want to get attached to a girl before he went to college. He spent his time kayakin`, sightin` birds, and studyin` marine life. And he never hung out with the wild bunch. He was the kind of guy who was goin` places."

"You had any other ideas about that doll skeleton?" I asked.

"I been thinkin` and thinkin`, but for the life of me, can't come up with any. You?"

I shook my head. "Not yet, but there has to be a message there."

"No doubt about that. Tomas was no dummy. He had something in mind."

"What do you know about the Day of the Dead?"

"Ugh, sounds dreadful. Not something I'd like to know about."

We stepped inside the bar and grill.

Like usual, the place was full of laughter and live music, but because the season was almost over, fewer customers.

Turning sideways we maneuvered around the pool table. Zen, I knew, would make for the back deck. That's where smoking was allowed. Zen no longer smoked, but the smell of burning tobacco was a lure. I stopped at the bar and ordered two drinks, motioning Zen forward.

The bartender was a cherub-faced, five-foot-two brunette who looked like she belonged at home studying for her high school exams. Although the physical resemblance wasn't close, I couldn't help but think of Lil, the former Bert's bartender I'd befriended last year. She had moved to Key West. Next season I might travel down to see her. Once I had painted Hemingway's house. The canvas now was gathering dust in a closet. I thanked the new bartender whose dangling earrings swept across the straps of her T-shirt. Holding the beers over my head, I weaved through the crowd, stopping when I heard my name called out.

"Jessie Murphy!"

27

I pivoted. To my surprise, it was Tomas's girlfriend, or ex-girlfriend, Caitlin Howard. In a bar the night you learn your boyfriend, even if he was an ex, was murdered? Really? She was standing beside a man who exuded an air of entitlement. Had to be the brother. The physical similarity was striking. Thinking that it would be easier for one person to manipulate through the crowd than for two, I went in their direction. Zen would have to wait for her beer.

"Hi." I stopped within an arm's length. "You're Caitlin, right?"

She had sad, puppy dog eyes.

Nodding once, she introduced the man who looked bored as her brother. She took a sip of her beer—a Dogfish Head Ale.

"I'm real sorry about Tomas," I said.

She ducked her head. Her brother drank from his bottle of Michelob before speaking. "That had ended. Caitlin was over him a long time ago."

"Oh? Your dad didn't seem to know that."

The young man snickered. "What dad knows anything about their kids? Caitlin ended that gig. The guy was a jerk."

"A jerk? In what way?" Although Caitlin had been the one to call me over, I noted that Brother Robert had taken control of the conversation. Caitlin merely kept her head down and wiggled her sandaled, toenail-polished toes. To me, this signaled that the girl was nervous.

"He was too aggressive, if you know what I mean. Caitlin is shy and inexperienced and that guy wanted more than she was willing to give. When she dropped him, he wouldn't take no for an answer. He kept calling her. I know, because I was in charge of her cell phone while they were abroad."

"Oh, that's right. She and your parents were on a technological-free vacation."

His lips tightened. "I guess that sums it up. Anyway, it's a terrible business, his death and all; but Caitlin and I are also relieved. The guy's persistence was starting to scare me. I began to worry that he might stalk her when she got back."

"That must have upset you."

Caitlin's right big toe rose. I registered the action.

"What?"

"Thinking your sister may be in harm's way must have made you real protective."

Caitlin's toe lowered.

He placed his beer bottle on the bar. "Sure. I was pissed."

Caitlin raised her head. I gazed into her child-like eyes and immediately was reminded of my ten-year-old northern neighbor. This was a kid, not a young woman. Of course her brother would be protective. A child in an adult body—in a beautiful woman's body. Had she and Tomas truly broken up?

"We . . ." Caitlin's hesitant voice was so soft it was almost drowned out by the crowd—but not quite. Her brother did that.

He took her elbow. "Don't listen to Caitlin. That's the problem. She doesn't know what's good for her. She's too innocent and easily taken advantage of. The guy was just after her money. That was apparent from the first time she brought him home."

Caitlin blinked rapidly. Her eyes were moist.

I felt sorry for her and began to wonder if the relationship had ended. The brother certainly wanted me to think it had. Interesting. I changed the subject. "I'll see you at the funeral tomorrow?"

Caitlin began to open her mouth. The brother applied pressure to her arm.

"Caitlin?" I stepped forward to better hear her.

Before she could speak, the brother continued. "She just wanted to tell you thanks for coming to the house and giving us the news. Right, Caitlin?"

Again, she ducked her head and nodded. "Yeah, thanks."

It was time to leave. Obviously, the brother wasn't going to let the girl do any talking. I'd have to get her alone. The girl wanted to talk. I could feel it. And I'd sure enough give her the chance. "Listen, I have to deliver this beer before it's hot

29

as a pancake on a skillet. See you two tomorrow at the funeral. And again, please accept my condolences."

I didn't look back until I got to the door. When I did, the siblings were gone.

Outside, Zen reached for her beer. "Who was that?" She grimaced at the bottle after her first sip, then gave me a disgusted look.

"Sorry, the next one will be colder."

"You're damn right it will be. I'll get it! So? Who were they?"

While I filled her in, Zen leaned back on the railing and crossed her legs. "I just knew it was the girl. She looks the part."

"What part?"

"A snooty well-heeled bimbo."

"I didn't get that feeling about her. And that rumor. Something's wrong with that too. Her dad said he liked the guy. Even hoped Tomas and his daughter would hook up permanently."

"And the bro?"

"He told a different story. He said Tomas was moving too fast on his sister and she dropped him."

"Tomas, move fast? Hah!"

"Maybe you didn't know everything about Tomas. Ever date him?"

Zen shook her head. "I guess I know men." She lit another cigarette.

I thought about her last boyfriend who she said was an angel. He'd slugged her before taking off. "Yeah, I guess you do know them," I said.

"They comin' to the funeral?"

"I suppose, but they didn't exactly say they were."

"Hope there ain't trouble. People have their own idea what happened to him."

"Ah, come on, they don't think the Howards killed him, do they? What would be the motive?"

30

Zen's lips tightened. "How about hatred of those who are not your kind? A half-Mexican dude wanting to marry a rich white chick. Ain't that ever been a motive for murder?"

"Listen, you get the word out that that family better not be harassed at the funeral or any time after. If I hear any word of anything like that going on, you can kiss this Private Detective, who really isn't a Private Detective anyway, goodbye. Got that?"

I hadn't been aware that my voice had gradually risen. But it had. I could tell by the startled faces around me and the fact that several men and woman stepped away and purposely refused to look our way.

A dark-skinned man in dreadlocks in a far corner beat a rhythm on a drum and sang a Jamaican tune. His words were of lost love and moving on. My mind drifted to my lover Will Rolins. More than once these past months I wasn't sure it had been wise to return to Matlacha where he'd been murdered last winter. But I had come and remained. I had continued to sketch and paint and I had three paintings in a local art gallery. I was starting to think about entering some local art contests. But listening to the music put me in a miserable mood. How long would it take for me to put Will totally to rest? A pelican flew in from a far island and landed on a piling near the colorful "Bert's" sign at the end of the dock. Hawk, my PI former boss up north, had cautioned me against coming. But he'd been wrong. I wasn't totally over my mourning, but coming to this place where Will and my memories were so vivid and beautiful had made me stronger, not weaker. I didn't believe in hiding from pain. Murphys jumped into the flames.

I caught the eye of a rough-looking, whiskered, stringy-haired man who was leaning against the outside railing, openly glaring at my girls. Narrowing my eyes, I crossed the dock and went in his direction. "Is there something about me that bothers you?"

The man, who looked like someone you might meet up with in a wrestling ring, waved his beer bottle and flipped his cigarette butt into the bay. His bear-hairy fingers came complete with dirt-encrusted, broken fingernails. He had a scar that parted his left eyebrow. "You talkin` to me?"

"Who do you think I'm talking to?" I held his attention like a soldier holds her aimed rifle.

I felt a rush of movement near my hip and glancing sideways almost came nose-to-nose with Zen. "Well, hi there, Russ. When did you get back in? I haven't seen you around here in a spell." She put her arm around my shoulder and squeezed. "I see you met my friend."

Russ took a cigarette out of his pack and gave Zen a hard grin. His eyes drifted back to me. By the time they reached my chest his grin had disappeared. His answer was a click of his tongue.

Zen took my elbow and steering me away and around the corner, guided me to another door that led into the front room of the bar. In a harsh whisper she said, "Hon, you don't know what's good for you. You don't want to mess with Russ. He don't take no guff from nobody."

I made out his broad back through the window. Another man was standing in front of him, talking. "Who is he, anyway?" I finished off my Guinness in one gulp.

"He's a crabber. There isn't anyone as mean as that guy. He's a cockhead."

I raised an eyebrow. "Don't you mean a dickhead?"

"Nah, cockhead. Name's Russ Beadle. He's a fourth-generation crabber. His gran-daddy smuggled drugs in from Colombia—the hard stuff. Russ spent ten years in a Texas prison for smuggling too. Drugs is in the family. Word is he inhales that white powder as if he were a pelican stealing chad."

Realizing Zen meant cokehead, not cockhead I opened my mouth to correct her, then changed my mind. Cockhead seemed to fit Beadle who straightened and gave the man near him a shove, knocking him off balance. The downed guy was helped up by another customer as Beadle leaned back against the railing again and lit another cigarette.

"A crabber, huh? Did he know Tomas?"

"Of course he knew Tomas. They worked together." Zen drifted away to swap Tomas stories with another local.

I kept my eyes on the muscle-bound cockhead crabber. I was one-twenty-five. He was close to two-eighty. A Super Bowl giant. I could take him in a split second with my secret weapon, karate. No doubt about it.

I added him to my suspect list.

6

That night, during my most vivid dream, sweat beads popped out on my forehead. I was waiting in line in front of the pearly gate. As my turn came, a female figure in a long Grecian-style dress who could have been Zen's sister, asked, "What or who would you like to be reborn as?" I placed my hands on my hips. "Isn't that something you should already know?" Poof!! My soul burrowed itself into the body of Alfred Hitchcock. "Oh great," I grumbled. "Now I'm bald! This is not what I was thinking!" The same voice, but this time from afar, spoke, "Smartasses get what they deserve." Eyes still closed, I grabbed another pillow and hugged it.

The following morning I sat in my room talking to Gar.

Six portraits I'd sketched in pencil were strewn across the palm tree-patterned bedspread: Tomas. The Howard siblings. Their parents. The cockhead.

"You agree, I'm a chicken, right?"

Gar said nothing, but that didn't stop the conversation.

"I know some people think I'm brave, being able to face a killer and all, but you and I know better, right?"

Number one example: I hadn't been able to take the step toward another full-blown relationship. I'd had a few dates, certainly felt sexual tension—like with Jay Mann. But it was a matter of courage, willingness to take the chance again to love. It was easier to resign myself to remaining a nun for the rest of my life than to start a relationship.

When I said this to Gar, I swore I heard him chuckle. "What's so funny?" I asked, removing his red-framed sunglasses. "You laughin` at me?"

But Gar refused to respond, so I replaced his glasses and paced, thinking about Tomas, the Howards, the whiskery crabber, Zen and Gator's request. I went to the window, opened the blinds and eyed the line of light beaming toward me across the pass. A pelican was sleeping on a piling. Seeing a pelican, Will's totem, had become easier, but still . . . I looked away. The water was peaceful like an unoccupied swimming pool and as clear as one left unattended with the pump turned off.

I picked up my iPhone from the sill. Turning my back on Gar, I made a call. "Hi John, it's me. Something's come up. Before you head out would you phone that friend of yours, Tim whatever-his-last name-is, and see if he can take over the management responsibilities until I return? If he can do it, you don't have to call me back. Just give him my cell phone number. I know you leave bright and early in the morning. But if he can't, please let me know and I'll try to find someone else. Enjoy yourself. You deserve it."

After ending the call I faced Gar again. "Oh, shut up!" I said. Then: "Grandma, you can just quit laughing too."

Half the time, it seemed like the woman who raised me, Grandma Murphy, followed my every move. Since early childhood when she took over my care-giving it had been her green eyes I first looked into every morning, her words I absorbed, her way of eating I mimicked, even her favorite beer I later learned to drink. My grandpa had died an early death. My dad was never part of my life. My mom had to work to support us. Grandma was my mom's and my salvation.

I spent the day sketching and relaxing, taking in the sun's rays for a couple of hours. But I felt antsy, anxious. I needed to do something to settle down. Leaving Gar to guard the room, grabbing my sketchpad, I got in my car and drove toward Pine Island to a place I knew I could relax and think.

Several cars idled in front of the building. I parked and went around the native potted plants. Normally the sea soothed me, but today there had been too many distracting boats on the water. I needed something else and I knew what it was—this quiet hidden sanctuary where I could sit alone and meditate without interruption. As I walked toward a bench near a pebbled labyrinth, I inhaled the powerful energy that drifted up from the ground.

Near the gazebo, people were meditating in a circle. Another small group of men and women were doing Chi Gong. Ducks, egrets, a great blue heron, and three turtles surrounded the pond. Towering bamboo swayed. Pelicans filled a grove of trees in the distance. I bent my head and continued on, believing no one would enter my space, trusting they felt my need for solitude.

I sat on the bench, folded my legs into the lotus position, and put my arms on my legs, palms up. Ever so slowly I sank down into my inner spring, staying there until I felt calmer, stronger, ready to face any speeding shark.

That night I slept like a newborn.

The next day I power walked my three miles before stopping and chatting a while with the Matlacha Candy King, Chris. He told me a story about how he believed the spirit of a deceased woman who had once had a grocery store in the building often visited his shop. As I left a pelican flew overhead and I felt Will's presence, a feeling that always gave me renewed belief in supernatural possibilities.

An hour later, thinking about Tomas, I dressed slowly. There was nothing easy about going to a funeral, nothing at all.

Over half of the mourners at Our Lady of the Miraculous Medal Church in Bokeelia were Mexican. I nodded at a striking, olive-skinned woman who seemed close to my mom's age. A blue scarf covered her hair and she wore a multi-colored sleeveless dress that showed off her thin arms. Our eyes locked and hers seemed to bore into me. I suddenly felt vulnerable, exposed, revealed. I shifted in my pew. She ducked her head. There was something about her that reminded me of my Grandma Murphy's psychic in Cambridge. I wondered if she could be one. She certainly appeared to be peering into some deep place inside me. My curiosity was piqued. My grandma would be so impressed if I told her I'd met a psychic down here. Nothing made me feel better than impressing Grandma Murphy. Sometimes I wished I could phone her. I used to try, but she refused to turn her hearing aid on. Answering a phone was something she just didn't do. As we filed out I searched for the woman in the blue scarf. But, she was being led through a side door by a younger woman, who by the profile, I guessed to be her daughter. I assumed I'd see them later. If I didn't, I'd have one less story to tell Grandma—one less chance for bragging rights.

After the service, everyone was invited back to the Moore house for food and drink. I rode with Zen and now-barefoot Gator in his rusty Dodge Ram pickup. Tomas was to be cremated and his ashes would be sprinkled into the Gulf from the family crabbing vessel with only the immediate family members onboard, so there would be no gravesite gathering.

Shorty and Mariana Moore lived north of Pine Island Center—a place that had once been called Tom's Town. Driving slowly with our headlights on and veering off Stringfellow Road, a long line of cars and trucks soon passed a new housing development with a dozen or so upscale homes and manicured lawns. Turning a corner, the pickup bumped onto a narrower, one-lane road. Twisting and winding through palmetto palms and land that looked as if it had once been a nursery, we followed a Chevy. Behind that car was a PT Cruiser. Behind that—another pickup, then a BMW. The Chevy pulled into a cleared piece of land at the west side of a house and parked. Gator pulled in beside them.

The green-shuttered home was a saddle-bag Cracker house—the type I admired most. Fronted with a full porch for cooling shade, the siding was unpainted, weathered cedar. The one-room deep, one-story building was kept off the ground by three-foot high cement-block pillars. A stone chimney towered above the steep roof at one of the gable ends. Somewhere through time another two rooms had been added to the original one—thus the house achieved the saddle-bag nickname. Pink bougainvillea dripped from a falling trellis on the far end of the porch. Two rustic, also unpainted rocking chairs trembled as Zen, Gator, and I ascended the steps while a scraggly dog of some unknown variety licked my hand.

Under a revolving ceiling fan, we paid our respects to Tomas's parents near the door. I was struck by the sight of the little girl of no more than eight who stood beside the Moores. I wanted to say something to her that would be meaningful, but what did one say to a child who had just lost an older brother she most likely adored? Instead, I took her hand, shook it and walked on in silence to mumble nothings to Zen and Gator who now had beads of sweat dotting their foreheads. I eyed the wall. It was completely covered with framed amateur watercolors of owls. In fact, figurines of owls were everywhere. My great aunt had a thing for chickens. Her house was filled with them. I guessed Mrs. Moore had the same thing for owls. I wondered who the artist was in the family, perhaps Tomas's little sister.

Soon the kitchen, overwhelmed by the odorous power of human sweat, became so oppressive that the crowd was pushed through the back door where the air was less cruel. A bevy of men nearly hid the beer keg from view. Lines of tables overflowed with platters of crab claws, shrimp, steamers, salads, cheese and crackers. A woman with a banjo and two men with guitars whom I recognized as The Fish & Tips, performed a southern tune. The woman singer had the voice of an angel. A long-necked white egret walked slowly toward a kid who was tempting it by wiggling a live shrimp in the air.

Spotting the keg, Gator excused himself. I was watching him fill three plastic glasses when a surprise guest blocked my view—the deputy who I had bumped into at the sheriff's office. I saw no escape, so held my ground. Zen was quicker on her star-studded, painted-toenail toes. She smirked at his smiling face and hurried away in the opposite direction. The advancing man stopped directly in front of me and offered me a clear plastic glass of beer.

"The sheriff ask you to be here?"

"Not at all. Tomas and I were friends. He taught me how to fish in these waters."

"Ah, I see." I scanned the crowd.

"You don't like me, do you?" His expression was one of amusement.

I blushed and caught his eye. "Should I?"

"Perhaps we should begin anew. Shall we?"

Oops. Sorry, Grandma. Give the guy a chance. Not all cops are bad guys. No snap judgments. I gave one quick nod.

"Hi, my name's Tobin Peterson. I was one of the deceased's fishing buddies. I also happen to be a police officer. And you?"

I accepted his outstretched hand. "I'm Jessie Murphy, a family friend. Nice to meet you. Tomas was a really cool guy."

Peterson cleared his throat. "Yeah, he sure was. I've never known anyone more focused on getting his undergraduate degree with high honors. In the two years we knew each other, I came to like him a great deal. In fact, two nights before his death he came to the Cape and we went for a drink. Something was bothering him. And it wasn't just that he had a cold."

"He had a cold?"

"Oh, yeah. He kept blowing his nose. If it had been anyone else I might have connected the action to sniffing coke, but no way with Tomas. Finding drugs in his place blew me away."

"I see," I said. "What was bothering him?"

He frowned and finished his beer. "I wish I knew. I believe he was going to tell me, but before he had a chance, we were interrupted by his girlfriend's brother."

The brother? "Really?"

"Yeah. He came into the bar, saw us and headed right for Tomas. I know, because I watched him enter the place. The brother's face went from calm to angry in thirty seconds. He and Tomas talked at the other end of the bar, then Tomas came back and told me he'd call the next day and left with him." He sounded wounded. "I didn't see him again."

"Of course you told the sheriff."

"Of course."

I sipped my beer, thinking. Peterson's story confirmed my hunch. I suspected the brother had a run-in with Tomas ever since I'd watched him with his sister—so over-protective— saying he thought Tomas might stalk her. Feeling a presence, I glanced to my right. It was Zen. Oh, oh. Zen had no liking for cops.

"You botherin' my friend?" Zen asked.

I almost laughed. Zen's expression was so icy cold it would chill a Tanqueray and tonic. Instead, I gave Zen a "don't be silly" grin as Tomas's parents headed our way.

Ignoring her, Peterson spoke briefly with the parents, nodded at me, and then backed away. I was left alone with the Moores and my redneck friend.

Shorty Moore was a tall, stout man whose broad chest and protruding stomach were too big for his suit jacket. His skin was weathered, his hair salt and pepper.

"Please, call me Jessie. As I told Zen and Jay, I'm not a private investigator. If it were me, I'd hire the real McCoy."

Shorty placed his hand on my shoulder. "I think we got that, my dear. It's your help we want."

"Well, all I can promise is to do the best I can. I'm sure Zen told you that I want my involvement kept secret. As far as all concerned, I'm just a family friend." This tactic had worked last year and I hoped it would work again.

"Don't worry, we aren't thick." He drew his wife near. "Mariana, tell this young woman what Tomas told you."

Mariana Moore was around five-foot-one. She had a fat-free body and muscular arms. Zen had told me that until recently Tomas's mother worked right alongside her husband in the crabbing business. Her eyes were red from crying, but her voice was steady as she spoke. "Tomas told me he was afraid."

Gator's words exactly.

"He refused to tell me why, but he came here looking for his dad and uncle. He seemed real worried. I tried to get him to wait for them. They'd gone off to talk to the guy they sell our catch to, but Tomas was too jittery and he didn't like me fussing over him. He took off on his motorcycle before I could do nothin' else."

"And when was this?"

"The night that he was . . ." She couldn't finish her sentence. She didn't have to.

Her husband continued for her. "He never found us. Me and Pepper, that's my brother, stopped in for a drink. When I got home, Mariana told me what happened and I went out looking for him, but I couldn't find him anywhere. I didn't get home until two. We got the call around three."

"So, he wasn't living here during spring break?"

Mariana shook her head. "No. He wanted his space. The woman who owned the kayaking tour place included a trailer in the deal if he'd be a guide."

"Where's the trailer located?"

"Behind the office in Matlacha. Just beyond that outdoor restaurant that keeps changing hands. It's easy to find. There's a stack of kayaks at the side of the building. I went there twice that night. The last time around ten thirty. He wasn't there. The woman, I think her name is Lori something or other, is here someplace." Shorty scanned the crowd. "That's her. The one with the bushy hair wearing the butterfly dress. You might want to talk to her."

41

"Do either of you have any idea of what or who might have frightened your son?"

"You can bet we're trying to come up with an answer for that, but so far, we're blank. Tomas wasn't the type to have enemies and we can't find anyone he talked to. I guess that's where you come in."

I got the feeling that Mariana was holding something back, but she didn't speak up.

I kept myself from sighing. "So, I hear you met his girlfriend?"

Mariana's expression brightened. "Cat! Ah, she was real nice."

Shorty frowned. "Nice, my eye! She dropped him like a two-day-old dead shrimp after she came here for supper."

"Tomas never said that. It's a lie," Mariana said. "They were in love. I could tell."

I concentrated on Tomas's dad. "If Tomas didn't tell you that they had broken up, what makes you think they did?"

"Do you see her here? Why else would she be absent? We haven't heard a word from her or her highfalutin family."

As a matter of fact, I hadn't seen any of the Howards at the funeral and certainly not here.

"That family thinks they're too good for the likes of us. Russ Beadle told me that girl split so fast that her sandals burnt rubber."

"Ah, Russ Beadle told you." Just one run-in with that cockhead and I knew I wouldn't put anything past him.

"That's right," Shorty said.

I had one more question. "Your wife said you went to talk to the buyer for your crab. Who was that?"

"I'm selling to the fish house in south Pine Island. They're fair enough."

"What's the name of the owner?"

"Toy Sorensen," Shorty said.

"Oh, and one more thing, does Russ Beadle work for you?"

"Beadle? Nah. He's too independent for that. He's his own crabber, always has been."

"But I heard Tomas and he worked together."

"Not that I know of," he said, looking puzzled.

I raised my brow at Zen. So much for that bit of information. Some people always get the facts wrong. It's a knack they have. Mixing up puzzle pieces and not being able to put them back together. As far as I knew, the rumor that Tomas and Caitlin had broken up could have begun with Zen, not Russ, not that she would admit it. But I would check the facts further. Maybe Tomas did work for Russ and his parents didn't know it.

I thanked them and after assuring me I'd get my first fee installment by Monday, the Moores began talking to other guests. By the size of the gathering, the Moore family was liked in the community. I checked out the crowd again. Very odd. I had been sure the Howards would attend. I wondered what had kept them away.

The woman in the pale-green, filmy dress with a large butterfly imprinted on the skirt moved toward the food table. Leaving Zen with Gator, who had just joined us, I drifted that way.

Within seconds, I knew that her name was Lori Sabal. She owned both the kayak touring business and a jewelry shop in Matlacha. She'd moved from Ohio ten years ago and except for the week before her mother's death, had never gone back. I guessed she was close to fifty.

"Tomas worked for you?" I asked as we filled our plates with seafood and salads.

"Yes. He loved giving tours. I'm going to miss him terribly." I could see she'd been crying.

"He liked the housing you gave him?" I said in a casual voice.

"Yes, he did, but it was only for spring break." Lori stepped away from the table. Her loop earrings touched her shoulders. "He was such a good worker and a kind young man. I still can't believe he's dead."

"I guess you knew he had a girlfriend."

"Sure. He talked about her on occasion."

"There's a rumor going around that they broke up."

"Yes, I know. I heard, but Tomas never mentioned it to me."

"Actually, just between you and me, his parents just told me he said he was of afraid of something, but he died before they found out what it was. Unfortunately, I hadn't seen him in quite some time. Know anything about that?"

"Hmm. No, I can't say that I do. He took two couples on part of the Great Blue Way the day he died. I didn't see him when he returned."

"Would you have the names of those people? Mariana just asked me to help her understand why he died. She's taking this real hard."

"The poor thing. I can't imagine losing my child like that. She's grasping at straws. I don't know their names, but they'd be listed in my ledger. Stop in tomorrow. The office is, of course, closed today." Her eyes darted to the right, she excused herself and strolled away.

By the time Chris showed up with his plate of sweets, it was well after four o'clock and I felt exhausted. Crowds are energy zappers for me. I don't do funerals or weddings well, having no gift for small talk and even less patience with total strangers. That is, unless I'm sketching or interrogating them. Crowded spaces defined my notion of sizzling purgatory. Flames shooting. Words nothing but gibberish. The whole place smelling of burnt flesh.

I chose a piece of peanut butter fudge from Chris's plate and to hide my dire mood smiled at him, but his attention was on the woman in the butterfly dress, Lori.

"Do you know her?" I asked.

"Of course. All Matlacha business owners know each other. The cops might want to ask her how well she knew Tomas."

"Really?"

44

"Yes, really. I'm not saying the feeling was mutual, but, oh there were feelings, no doubt about that. I saw them together once."

Of course I immediately speculated on whether Tomas could have been killed because of unrequited love. I just couldn't help myself. But when I tried to get Chris to elaborate he said he had no other information.

I could smell coffee. After my dose of sugar, a cup sounded more than fine. I took Chris's arm and while chatting, guided him toward the coffee pot that had just been set on the checkered tablecloth. The candy tray Chris carried was empty by the time we reached the pot.

When a man backed into me, I grunted.

"Oh, excuse me."

"No problem at all." I held out my hand. "Jessie Murphy, a family friend."

"Ty Chambers, a school chum." He ducked his head. "I was just leaving. Nice to meet you," and he was gone.

"Know him?" I asked Chris.

"Nope."

I watched the young man's retreating back, knowing I'd be seeing him again. Mariana Moore walked into view. Her eyes were on Ty Chambers' back too. I was sure of it. I typed the name into my brain.

"I was going to tell you this later," Chris said, "but, now's as good a time as any. The sheriff brought a skeleton doll to the shop today."

"Oh, really?"

"Yeah. Looked just like the photo you showed me. She asked lots of questions about Tomas."

"Interesting."

"Even asked for my alibi the night Tomas was killed."

"And do you have one?"

He dropped two sugar cubes into his paper coffee cup and reached for a plastic spoon. "I was playing bridge."

"What else did she ask?"

He raised his eyebrow. "Very PI behavior."

I blushed and warned myself to be subtle.

Chris continued. "Wanted to know if you and Tomas were having a relationship. Seemed to think you were."

I choked on my coffee, then squeezing my nostrils, set down the cup. "And you told her?"

"Honey, I had to be honest. I said I had no idea."

"Really? REALLY?"

Chris inspected the crowd before speaking, "I don't like to judge people, but in my estimation that woman doesn't think much of Mexicans. Where do we get our officers of the law anyway?"

I told him I had met her and had come to the same conclusion. He excused himself and headed for his van to refill his tray.

At least I knew now that by delivering the skeleton doll I'd achieved action from the sheriff. That was something. I wondered who else she had questioned and what other angle she might be working on other than me killing a young lover who might have done me wrong—the same conclusion I had jumped to with Lori. If I were lucky, people would keep me informed. I just hoped I could keep the sheriff and others unaware of my investigation. I really didn't want her or anyone crawling down my back like many legged centipedes in heat.

I nodded at Gator and Zen and they came my way. "Ready to leave?" Zen asked. "Gator needs to get back."

I remembered the woman I hoped or had a feeling was a psychic—the one that was going to put me on a pedestal in Grandma's little black book, I glanced around, but no luck. Drat.

We said our farewells and walked around the house. In the truck, I asked Gator to describe exactly what he had found when he discovered Tomas's body. "Please leave out no detail, starting with the door. Was it locked or unlocked?"

"Ah, come on," Gator said. "It was unlocked, of course. How else would I have gotten in?"

Rolling my eyes at Zen who sat between us, I left the question unanswered. Anyone knew even a pea-brain could get into a locked trailer or a house, for that matter.

"So, I pulled the screen door open."

"The screen door?"

"Yep. The other door was standing open."

"Okay, go on."

"And called his name. When I got no answer, I stepped inside." Gator started the engine and shifted into reverse, backing up slowly.

"What did you see?"

"Hmm, well, there were maps spread across the sofa and two half-finished bottles of Dogfish Head Ale and a candle on the table, and . . ."

"Unfinished? Are you sure?"

"Sure. You bet I noticed. I wouldn't let good beer like that go to waste!" He looked from me to Zen and shrugged.

"Two chairs?" I asked.

"What?"

"Were there two chairs at the table or one? Did it look like two people might have drank the beers or just Tomas? Or were there more chairs?"

"Good thing you said "look like" `cause I couldn't know. But there were two chairs and one bottle was set in front of each."

"Then," Zen said in an excited voice, "we can deduce that two people were there and for some reason, didn't finish their beers. And if they didn't finish, then something made them stop. Right?"

"Deduce?" Gator said, giving Zen the eye.

Zen grinned and raised her chin high.

"Well, done, Watson," I said. "Of course, they maybe had just had enough beer and left them unfinished."

"Don't be ridiculous, hon! No one does that." Zen laughed. "Maybe I should be your sidekick. I'd be a good one, don't you think?"

Oh, sure, all I need is a "get-the-facts-all-wrong" helper. To Zen I said, "I work best alone, but if I need to consult anyone, I'll sure come to you."

Satisfied, Zen smiled so wide her gums were visible. I asked Gator to continue.

"Anyways, when I turned toward the bathroom, I tripped over a damn book and bout broke my neck."

"A book? Did you get the title?"

Gator looked around Zen and gave me a "you've got to be kiddin'" look. "Oh, sure, love, I bent right down and read the damn title! I did that `cause of course I knew knowin` it would be important later! Woman, get real! I was just trying to find Tomas to have him join us for a beer. It was a big sucker of a thing and it was open to a page showing the inside of a body— thought of Moby Dick and that damn whale, is what I thought of."

"Sorry," I said.

"The drugs, it was in the morning paper, so guess you know about them, were covered by one of those maps. When I tripped over the book, I touched a corner of the map and it slid off uncovering the bag of coke."

"And you were sure it was coke?"

"Oh, yeah. No doubt about that." The pickup hit a bump, making both Zen and me grab the dashboard. "Sorry, that pothole's big enough to fish in. Bet it's home to a trout or two. Hang onto your drawers." Gator swerved to the right to miss another hole. "Someone needs to bring a load of gravel out here." He spun the wheel, barely missing taking a slice out of a trunk of a palm tree.

Zen gave Gator a disgusted look. "It's not like you could slow down or nothin`."

Gator winked at me. I put my foot on the dashboard. When the front wheels lurched onto pavement, I sent up a prayer of thanks and asked Gator to describe what he found in the bathroom.

Gator was hesitant. "Are you sure? It weren't pleasant."

"Please. Any detail might give a clue. Zen, do you mind?"

Although her face had paled, Zen said she could take it, so Gator continued. "Well, I first thought the door was locked and he was in there, 'cause I couldn't budge it, so I yelled his name again, but when he didn't answer, I tried the knob and pushed. No go. With my shoulder against the wood, I shoved the door open, and well, he was sitting slumped in the corner. His feet must have been against the door. He didn't have a shirt on. I rushed to him, but I knew he was, well, you know. There was . . . blood everywhere."

No one spoke for several minutes. "Did you see anything else in that room?"

"Like what?"

"I don't want to put any ideas in your head. Just think back. Did you notice anything unusual?"

Gator turned the truck south onto Stringfellow. Zen shifted on the seat. I slid closer to the door. When we came to Tom's Town, Gator said, "Well, as I think on it, there was one odd thing."

Zen and I spoke at the same time. "What!?"

Gator puffed his chest out. "Well, first I thought it was one of those statues folks buy to put in their yard. You know the kind—made of metal and lookin' so real that you want to touch 'em." He hesitated, lighting another cigarette.

"Go on," I urged.

"Well, that thing walked right out of the corner and almost made me swallow my tongue." He scratched the whiskers on his left cheek. "That was the biggest blue heron I've ever seen. I mean, what was that bird doing in that trailer? I'd left the door ajar and I'll be damned if it didn't walk right past me and out it went."

I let out the air I'd been holding. Zen wiggled her whole body. "Well, that isn't a clue. A bird isn't a clue. We got birds everywhere."

I settled back in the seat. I knew better than to disregard any detail. Sometimes the most far-fetched thing could make all the difference in the world in solving a mystery. Besides, a great blue walking around someone's home? How cool was that? I could already feel an urge to sketch rising. One never knew what would inspire my desire to pick up my drawing pencils.

"So Tomas didn't have one as a pet?"

"Not that I ever knew of," Gator said, switching on the radio.

"You got any ideas about what that skeleton might mean?"

"Wish I did, but I'm drawin` a blank."

No mention of a weapon. Apparently the killer had taken it with them. At least, it apparently wasn't in sight.

Zen put her head back on the seat and hummed to Johnny Cash's *I Walk the Line*. I realized I knew little about Gator. Best to know about people I associate with, especially those I might like to consider a friend who had my back.

"You got any family, Gator?" Cash's raspy voice almost drowned out my words.

"One sister. We haven't spoke for years. She's a doc up north. Crazy as a rabid coon. Folks think of me as a brainless, slithering animal just `cause of how I look. Her, in that burb she lives in with her fancy clothes, she's the queen of the family." His dimples deepened with his broad grin.

I chuckled. "Apparently they haven't asked you about the local pirates." I'd found out last year when investigating Will's death that Gator was an expert on that subject.

Gator tapped the horn lightly. "Guess everyone needs some kind of specialty. What about you? You got family?"

"My mom lives in Boston, but I was raised by my grandma. No siblings."

Gator sniffed. "Your dad not in the picture?"

I set back on the seat so he could no longer see my face. "Died when I was a kid. Like I said, my grandma raised me." I watched the landscape, my thoughts returning to Tomas. He left a package with Gator two days before his death containing a religious symbol. Why didn't he just leave words of explanation with Gator? Tomas had to have known his life was in danger. Did he fear Gator would open the package and read a note he left?

"Hey!" Zen said in a hurt voice.

I glanced her way. "Yeah?" So did Gator.

"Don't anyone want to know about me?"

"Nope," Gator and I said in unison.

Minutes later, arriving in Matlacha, Gator pulled up in front of the inn. The curls of his long beard tossed to the blare of music. The fingertips of his left drummed the steering wheel.

Saying goodnight, I climbed out. Tomorrow, I would go to the St. James fish house and ask some questions. What I knew about Tomas's family business, I could put into the lid of a tiny paint tube. Knowing about Tomas's lifestyle in the islands should help me create a profile and hopefully kick open doors concerning his murder.

7

Ten a.m. The fish house was on Palm Drive, south off Stringfellow Road. As I drove past a gated condo community I thought perhaps my GPS had malfunctioned. Why would a business be situated in a residential area? Duh! Obviously it was there first.

Stacked crab traps. Fifty-gallon barrels. Metal shipping containers. Plywood leaning against a pile of plastic bags. A two-toned, one-story building painted lavender with an air conditioner sticking out the small window near the entrance. All this presented a scene of a no-holds-barred, get-in-your-face working environment.

Stepping out of my car, I slammed my door. A man in overalls and white boots sporting a long braid down his back was hunkered down working on a boat trailer. As I neared, sketchbook in hand, he looked up. "Yeah?"

I hesitated. "Is the owner around?"

He gave a quick nod and motioned toward the building. "Toy's in the office. Don't worry about the dog. He don't bite." He returned to his work.

I thanked his back and went in that direction. An animal that looked more wolf than dog lay on a bed of ice near the door. The beast raised his snout and stared right into my eyes. His pupils were solid black buttons of pure iron. The irises were copper rods. His expression showed he knew who was in the position of power. And it wasn't me.

Despite what the man said, having a healthy respect for any animal that weighed about the same as I did, I froze in mid-step. I didn't care if the dog's tail wagged, I knew I wasn't moving. Without turning my head, I glanced toward the door and the spot where the man had been, hoping someone noticed my dilemma: Woman with unreasonable, but very real fear of dog in vicinity. Help. Not that I said anything out loud. It seemed my vocal chords were also frozen. This kind of thing didn't happen often to me. But when it did, it did.

Floor boards crackled. Someone was coming. I could only wish for a miracle.

"What can I do for you?" The male voice was gruff, but welcoming.

Keeping my attention on the dog, I squeezed out a "Hi."

The man came down the steps and leaned down to pet the dog's ears. "This is Blue. He wouldn't hurt a flea."

"How about a woman?" Oh, I believed him all right, but I still did not move.

He didn't chuckle. "Go on around him. I'll put him in the back room."

Apparently there was an outside entrance, because the guy walked around the building with Blue.

I cleared my throat, straightened my shoulders and pretended that no one else had noticed my obvious fear of the dog, especially the person who'd been working on the trailer who now stood to my right grinning like a kid with a Popsicle in his hand.

I was probably the only "kind of" PI in the area who was more comfortable with a paint palette and brushes in her hand than asking questions to solve a crime. I was also most likely the only one who'd been chased by a mad dog when I was eight. Turning my head regally (well, whatever) I gave the man a broad smile, forgiving him for thinking of me as a silly female.

Head high, I strolled to the steps and taking them two at a time, went inside. The man who had rescued me entered from the back. He was over six-feet tall and had a Paul Bunyan physique. "I'm Toy Sorenson." Watching him lower himself was like watching a king take his throne.

Toy? This large guy? Go figure. I thought of asking him how he got his nickname, but decided against it. I put out my hand, "I'm . . ."

"I know who you are. Take a seat."

Taken aback, my smile dissolved as I sat. Had the word gotten out I was investigating Tomas's death?

"You're the artist friend of the Moores, right?"

I relaxed and assured him that I was.

"A dreadful thing, losing Tomas like that. His killer needs to be dipped in feathers and fried in hot oil."

"I couldn't agree more. Mariana asked me to talk to you. She knew you were close. The paper said drugs were found in his trailer. She wants to know what you know about that."

Toy let out a resounding volume of air. "Yeah, well, Tomas was a hard worker. Honest. Smart. Trustworthy. Taking drugs? I don't believe it." His words drifted away. He seemed to be attempting to keep emotion out of his voice, but it had seeped in.

"I know that this is difficult." I was amazed at how my mind kept connecting this guy with British royalty. It wasn't his worn blue jeans or stained white T-shirt or white, fish-smelling boots, that was for sure. Yet, I couldn't help feel like I was a visiting subject in his court.

His head raised and his eyes met mine. The color and expression reminded me of Blue. If I were the killer, I wouldn't want to run into this guy. He looked like he could break a neck with one hand or pay someone to do it. But there was also a quality about him that made me like him. He seemed like a guy who would tell it straight.

"Yeah, well, I never had a son, but if I had—I'd want a carbon copy of that kid. It's hard to accept that he's gone." His eyes glistened.

I was touched. The man had a loving heart. He rubbed his right hand over the hole in the knee of his jeans. "Well, I guess it's okay to tell you this. Tomas asked me to keep my mouth shut and I did, while he was alive. He didn't want his folks to know. He was moonlighting with Beadle whenever he could. He needed the extra money and he was afraid if he told his folks they'd go and borrow some and he sure didn't want that."

"I see. Well, that was certainly thoughtful on Tomas's part. What can you tell me about Beadle?"

Toy made a "fuh" sound, leaving off the final consonant. "That egomaniac? He plays half his cards off the bottom of the deck. I warned Tomas to stay away from him. But he needed the money too bad."

"Would Tomas have any reason to fear him?"

"Everybody has a reason to fear that guy. If I were a cop, I'd focus my attention on him. He's got a killer's instinct. Listen, when you tell Mariana about Beadle, make sure Shorty isn't around. He's a hothead. Don't know what he'd do with that news. Losing your son can make you do things that you normally wouldn't do. "

I assured him that I would leave it up to Mariana to tell her husband.

I took out my cell phone and showed him the photo of the skeleton. He said it meant nothing to him.

"Tomas gave this to Gator all wrapped up and said if anything happened to him, to give it to me."

He stared at the photo. "Huh."

"Are you sure it means nothing to you?"

He took too much time to say no. Way too much time.

"Would you have any idea who might know something about it?"

His lips worked. "I guess I'd ask his folks. They know him the best. That all? I got work ta do."

Still not convinced that Toy was clueless, I pocketed my phone.

55

A thin man in overalls with sandy hair who looked to be in his mid-forties walked out of the inner office. Toy introduced him as Shark.

Apparently the locals got a kick out of giving themselves humorous handles: Gator, Zen, Shorty, Pepper, Cockhead, Toy, and now Shark. I wondered what they called me when my back was turned—Quickwalker—a woman sidestepping from a close relationship faster than a crab on land seeks water. I reckoned everyone knew about how Jay Mann had been trying to get in my boxer shorts ever since I returned to Matlacha.

Toy nodded toward Shark. "Watch out for this guy. He's a crabby son-of-a-gun," he said good-naturedly as he stood and excused himself. "You need anything else, here's my card. You can call me at any time. I got ta git out to the dock." And he slammed the door on the way out.

I was startled by Toy's quick departure. I wanted to ask him about the great blue heron that Gator saw in Tomas's trailer. That was an odd thing—that bird. There just might be a clue there.

I looked at Shark.

"You ever been on a crab boat?" he asked.

"No. Afraid not. I don't know much about crab fishing."

"Want to go out?"

The abrupt question startled me. Why the sudden invitation? We stood eye to eye. Shark looked like his nose had been broken. He took a piece of paper out of his pocket and read it. His expression was a study in grim.

"Might learn a thing or two," he mumbled.

"When?"

"Tomorrow."

"Well… I was thinking I need to find Russ Beadle." Besides, you look a tad bit on the scary side.

"Won't find Beadle around till next week. He left for Key West this mornin`."

"Oh."

56

That Beadle had fled the area was like pointing a spotlight at himself.

Shark apparently assumed my silence was a "no"; he started to go around me. "Just a thought," he grumbled.

Instinct told me to go and if there was one thing Grandma was insistent on it was to follow my instinct. I swiveled. "No, I mean in fact, that's a great idea. What time do you leave?"

"Seven, I guess. Here. I keep my boat at my house." He reached into his bib pocket and pulled out a glossy, full-color business card with a crab picture filling the space, along with his name, address, and phone number.

A woman with brunette hair hurried out of the inner office, heading straight for Shark. "Hey! How come you never invite me to go out on your boat? How come you're inviting her?" She tossed me a look that said I wasn't worth the trouble.

"Guess you need to get up on the right side of the bed." Shark walked out with a wave of his hand and no backward glance.

I ducked my head and hightailed it for the door. Staying in a room vibrating with hostility never appealed to me.

I was almost to my car when Blue came bounding in my direction. I grabbed the handle, tore open the door and shut it as Blue settled his front paws just below the driver window which you can bet was closed. This junk yard dog wasn't growling or anything. Just looking. Really looking. Like BIG dogs tend to do, especially those who aren't far from living in the wild, tend to do.

"Nice poochie," I said, checking my heart for a missed beat. As I shifted gears, Blue jumped down. I looked toward the building. The woman stood in the doorway, arms crossed in front of her chest. A smile played on her lips. Blue ran to her. I gave the woman the finger and reversed the car. "Seaweed," I muttered. I was thinking a much nastier word, but I kept it for my own pleasure.

For several reasons as I drove toward Matlacha, I began having second thoughts about my decision to spend a whole day out on a boat with a complete stranger. I looked in the rearview mirror. Listen, kiddo, you've been told more than once when you worked for Hawk that you were one of those women who strove to please at the expense of your own well-being.

That you have trouble saying no is a given. Besides, you really should be staying land side and questioning other people, not learning details about crabbing that hardly could be listed as investigative work.

Russ Beadle should be your focus right now. Even though he split, you could gather information about him, find out if he had a record.

I pushed down on the gas pedal and passed a slow-moving car. And what if the crabber is kinky? Your swimming skills will take you about the length of two swimming pools. And performing karate on a boat might be just a bit beyond your skill level. Comprendo?

With my mind still not made up, I inched the car into a narrow parking space near the inn. Good thing I could care less if my car were scraped by another vehicle. There was little chance that it wouldn't be in these tight quarters. Pushing the car door open, I barely fit my body between the open spaces. One thing about Matlacha, parking was a joke. But at least there weren't meters like my neighborhood in Cambridge. Remaining sideways, with arms raised toward the cloudless sky, I danced my way to the front of the cars, turned right and headed for the inn.

A sea breeze wafted across the pass, relaxing me. Nothing, absolutely nothing made my muscles relax more than the knowledge I had a sea view, something I could never afford in the Boston area. Too bad it was so hot and humid in Florida in the late spring and summer and there were so many no-see-ums. Without those factors, I'd think seriously about moving here permanently.

By the time I reached my room, I had decided to cancel out on the crabbing trip. It was too bizarre of an idea for me to spend a day on a boat with a rough-looking guy I'd said only a couple of sentences to when I really should be investigating Tomas's death. An hour, maybe. But a whole day? Nah. I pulled his more than fancy, dancy business card from my breast pocket and made the call. Heck, at the very least, this guy was a grouch. Why would I want to spend time with someone named Shark? I tapped my foot as the phone rang.

Then: "Happy Birthday. Happy Birthday. Happy Birthday to you . . . ou . . . ou . . . ou!"

My eyes widened. Was I hearing things? Wasn't this Shark? The guy who'd left the office with his head bent toward the ground? The man who was so glum?

The song merrily continued, then stopped.

"Uh, this is Jessie Murphy, the woman you asked to go out crabbing with you."

His laughter was throaty. "Oh, crap! I thought you were my daughter. It's her birthday. Ah, I see, the first three numbers are the same. Sorry about that. What can I do for you?"

What kind of guy sang to his daughter like that? One I didn't need to worry about. That's what kind. I asked for directions to his house and pocketed the phone, still grinning. I reckoned this guy would have plenty of information about Beadle. Okay, so I was justifying my decision. I did so love being on the water.

I unlocked the inn room door. Gar sat on the nightstand facing the entrance.

"Gar, guess what? I'm going crabbing tomorrow. Can you believe it?"

Of course, then I knew I was in trouble. What did you wear to go crabbing? Long pants and a long-sleeved shirt would make good sense. Clothes to protect me from the sun. I smiled. It was Tuesday. All clothes at the thrift store were half price on Tuesdays and Saturdays.

But first, a bowl of prize-winning chowder at the Perfect Cup complete with a clientele of locals who were sure to have info about Russ Beadle. I left my room whistling. It was twelve thirty p.m.

8

Entering the café was like walking into a beehive of happy worker bees. The sound of voices created a buzz that made my ears ring. Inspecting the room and seeing no one I recognized I took a table for two near a half-wall separating the room near the door from another eating area. The waitress, Sal, weaved toward my table, took my order, and then sauntered away. The front door opened and I grinned.

Luke Abbot, the owner of the gallery that showed my work, spotted me and headed my way. His face was chiseled out of granite. His flowered cotton shirt showed off his broad shoulders. His white shorts made his muscular legs seem a deeper tan. He was the kind of guy who made a woman quickly inhale and I was no exception. But the great thing was that he wasn't high on ego. He seemed to accept his looks like I accepted the gift I was given to paint—as a lucky draw of the cards.

"May I join you?" His blue-green eyes sparkled.

"Absolutely. Thought you were in New York."

"Thought you'd be on the road."

"Touché."

Sal dropped by and Luke ordered a cup of chowder and bottle of water. He leaned his arms on the table. "I heard about Tomas."

"Yeah."

"You're not getting tangled up in this, are you?"

"Nah," I lied. I thought I'd show him the skeleton, but changed my mind. If I did that, he'd know I had my PI hat on.

Sal delivered our soup and bottles of water and shared her pride with Luke about her fifth-grade daughter. She had won a prize for her art. Luke congratulated her and suggested she bring her daughter with some of her work to his gallery. Sal left with a broad smile on her face.

I wanted Luke's take on Beadle, so . . . "I met a perfect subject for a painting at Bert's."

Luke grinned. "There's no end to material for a painter on this island."

"Yeah, but this guy is ideal. I mean, totally golden." Classical music drifted in from the radio in the fudge shop next door. A sun faded poster behind Luke's head advertised March's Mullet Toss. A dull ache entered my head threatening to explode into a full-blown headache. This often happened when I was blatantly lying. Catholic guilt residue, no doubt.

"So take time to sketch him before you leave. I love your portrait work." He nodded at a man who before looking at me. "What's his name?"

"Russ Beadle."

I wasn't prepared for Luke's reaction. His face paled a couple of shades. His spoon remained frozen in front of his open mouth. He blinked several times not catching my eye. Then, as if he knew his reaction was radical, he carefully placed his filled spoon back into his bowl, took his napkin off his lap and wiped his lips before speaking. "Ah, my dear, this is not a person you want to sketch. In fact, this is not a person you want anything to do with. This is a person to avoid."

I ran my gaze around the room noting that no one seemed to be paying attention to our conversation. If someone had been watching Luke, they might have thought I had delivered some very bad news.

Adopting my most innocent, mischievous expression I said, "Do tell."

He scratched behind his ear. "You are such an imp at times. Sometimes I think you're the most naïve, innocent woman I know. Eat your soup, woman."

"Oh, no you don't. What's the dirt on my future subject?"

His lips worked like an erratic toy clown with a damaged jointed movable jaw. "I wasn't kidding when I said you should stay away from this guy."

I said nothing.

His eyes narrowed. He obviously couldn't be more serious. "Stay away from him, Jessie. And that's an order. I like my artists to remain safe so they can continue to follow their hearts."

An order? He's giving me an order. Eww. Bad idea. It's a good thing he's such a good friend. I can forgive him. One doesn't order a Murphy woman around, especially if the demand is coming from a man. Once I rose above my urge to bristle and make a quick more than rude retort, I lowered my head and swallowed hard. I'm really not an airhead. Where Russ Beadle was concerned, err on caution.

I'd definitely have Hawk do a background check on Beadle.

I dropped the topic. Luke said he was leaving for New York the next morning and would be gone for a month.

I returned to my room to think and make a plan.

9

The next morning Shark stepped out from the corner of his house and motioned for me to park beside a pickup. He wore a hat with an extra flap that went from the tip of his ears around the nape of his head. Large sunglasses. A pair of rubber overalls covered his jeans and pink T-shirt.

The house was a modest one-story canal home. Crab traps lined the south side. The screened-in flat-roofed lanai or porch (as we called them up north) was hidden from view by a fence of large flowering hibiscus.

The flat-bottomed, twenty-some-foot wooden boat was tied to two pilings. It appeared the floor was made of plywood and I suspected the frame was too. The wood was coated in a bluish film that I assumed had been caused by the sun and weather. A large wooden box divided the steering station from the bow. A cooler was squeezed in between the front of the console and the box.

Shark jumped on board, tossing me a backward glance. "I guess I told you this wasn't no pleasure cruise," he said.

Ignoring his comment, I tossed my bag on board and ignoring his outstretched hand, climbed in. "I didn't expect it to be."

He stepped over an anchor, started the ninety-horsepower outboard and shifted the boat into gear. We putted down the canal, passing everything from a fifty-five-foot schooner to twenty-foot day sloops, to a Hatteras tied up to docks. Leaving the canal and houses behind, Shark increased the boat's speed, causing a small wake. I pulled out my drawing pad. A speedboat zipped past. Our boat rocked. I grabbed the side. My stomach gurgled.

"Damn fools," Shark said.

"Mind if I draw you?"

"Nah. My mug is on postcards," he said. "Guess I'm used to it being seen."

Time passed in silent companionship as Shark pulled in crab traps, dumped the catch into buckets and onto ice. Then he re-baited and tossed the traps overboard while I sketched. I began wondering if coming had been a wise decision. What did I expect to learn that would help me find Tomas's killer out here with Shark?

Pelicans, looking for an easy breakfast, swarmed the boat. I began to sketch one of them.

"Hey!" Shark yelled. He grabbed the offending pelican's beak and flung the bird toward the bow. The bird landed with a thud, shook its head, and then flew away—but apparently undaunted, circled and returned to rejoin the rest of the following flock.

My shocked exclamation of "Oh!" seemed to go unnoticed.

Yanking off his glove, Shark inspected the skin between his index finger and thumb. He put his hand to his mouth and sucked, and then lowered it. "Things aren't always as they appear to be." He slipped on his glove. "Like those pelicans everyone is always fawning over. Put temptation in front of them and they can be real mean critters." He reached in his bait box, pulled out a fish and gave it a toss. It landed in the mouth of the attacker bird he had just mistreated. I watched the peace offering slide down the bird's throat before returning my attention to Shark.

"Like you, for instance. You're more than a friend of the Moore family. You're investigating his death."

I caught his look. "Says who?"

"Oh, don't worry. I'll keep it to myself. I just know." He sat. "Tomas was a great kid. Everyone loved him, but something happened to him after he went off to college."

"Like what?"

Shark maneuvered the boat to a new location before responding. "Don't know, but it did. Trust me."

"What about Russ Beadle? Do you think he has a connection with Tomas's death?"

"Oh, lots of people think so. Toy does. That's why Beadle took off so quick, I reckon. But I'm not so sure. Guess that's part of your job, huh?"

"Maybe what happened to him was that he fell in love," I offered. "Love can change a person."

"That ain't the kind of change I saw in Tomas."

"Can you explain what you mean?"

Shark took island time inspecting the circling pelicans. When he spoke, he took off his cap. "Just like them pelicans, every creature has a dark side," he said. "When Tomas left the island he was an innocent. When he came back, he had something in his craw. He was angry. Discontent. He looked, well, just say he looked like he was an unhappy man."

An image of Ty Chambers, his college friend, formed. I wondered what he would know.

A yacht flew by creating a wake that rocked the boat. Shark swore and gave them the finger. Seasick prone, I blanched and steadied myself.

In the distance six kayakers paddled for an island.

Shark spat in the water. "He shouldn't of taken that job with Beadle. Everyone warned him to stay away from him, but he wasn't listening."

"What do you know about his girlfriend?"

"All I know is what I hear, that she broke up with him. And, well, she might have had more of a reason than folks know. That kid was steerin` for trouble. Now, I ain't trying to bad mouth him or nothin`. I just had the feeling he was involved in something he shouldn't have been."

66

"You think he was involved in something illegal?"

Shark pulled out another trap, dumped out the crabs, baited it, and then said, "Just don't let everyone tell you that that kid wasn't capable of doing bad. Maybe he wasn't once, but, well, I think you just have to find out what he was up to this spring break, 'cause I'm darn well sure, something was up."

I looked out over the calm water. Knowledge could change a person, no doubt about that. And change could be good or it could be evil.

I opened my cell phone and showed him the skeleton.

He scrunched up his eyebrows. "What's this about?"

"Tomas left this for me without a note of explanation in case something happened to him. Have any idea why he would do that?"

"Looks like a religious symbol."

"That's what I was thinking."

He gave me a stern look. "You best solve this case quick. That's a Mexican cult doll. Tomas's mom is Mexican. She and the rest of the family might be next in the line to be murdered."

I blanched. "Come on. That's quite a stretch."

But was it? Shark was right. Tomas's mom was Mexican. This was a Mexican symbol. Jesus! The whole family could be at risk. His little sister's face came into view. Damn.

Shark's tone hardened even more. "There's something going on that's got everyone nervous. You need to find out what it is before anyone else gets hurt." He turned his back to me.

"The sheriff said . . ."

"The sheriff? You in cahoots with that woman?"

Whoops. I realized I'd made a mistake.

With a look of disgust on his face, he yanked up a flattened trap and swore under his breath. "See this? This is what those fool boaters do to my business. These traps cost thirty bucks a pop to replace. Do those rich folks care? Hah!

Does the law do anything about it? Nah!" Untying the damaged trap he dropped it on the floor.

The sun was high in the sky. I slid onto the deck to avail myself of the small amount of shade that the shadow of the box provided. Shark took a long swig of Gatorade, unwrapped a sandwich, and opened a package of chips while I unzipped my plastic bags. My water was already warm, but it went down just fine.

Shark began to talk about the vacation he and his wife were going to take up north with other crabber families.

"What do you do with your traps while you're gone?"

He broke a potato chip in two before popping it into his mouth. "Leave them right where they are."

"All one hundred and fifty of them?"

He shrugged again.

"I'd think you'd worry about poachers."

"Last time a poacher was caught, he was found butt naked tied to mangrove roots on one of those islands out there. Had been there for days. Word gets around."

Whoa. I could think of better ways to get a tan.

Shark finished his sandwich and started the outboard.

I gazed across the water. I could never look out over such an expanse of sea without thinking about the creatures that lived there. Grandma, who loved anything turtle, made me aware of other living beings from the time I was old enough to have a pet goldfish. And now I found myself thinking about the evil that nobody would name, just as Shark refused to do.

Below this boat there existed a teeming world of its own. The creatures of the sea were endangered, threatened by overfishing, phosphates, and infringing development. I had a natural affinity for anything endangered and I felt I had at least some small sense of what it must be like to feel vulnerable in the path of progress. I couldn't solve those millions of manmade transgressions, but I thought that maybe I could solve Tomas's murder.

"I was wondering, what's a Florida crabber's worst enemy?" I asked.

Shark looked right and then left. "Other crabbers. Like crabs trapped in a bucket, when one tries to climb out, the others pull him down."

I remembered what the sheriff had said: Most murder victims were killed by family or friends. Was Tomas murdered by a jealous local who resented his desire to get a higher education? I began to draw Tomas's face, then the cockhead crabber, Russ Beadle.

"Shark?" I yelled over the engine noise.

"Yeah."

"Why did you invite me onboard? You could have talked to me anywhere."

He gave me an assessing look. "Not so many evil spirits or listening ears out here."

A pelican swooped low. Shark looked out over the horizon. I studied his profile. This was a captain in control, a lord assessing his kingdom, an old salt; a man who knew who he was and where he should be. I picked up my pencil again and we motored on, him crabbing, me sketching. The sun, the warming arms of a mother. The water, the milk from her breasts. If only Grandma Murphy had met this man.

Until . . . I pushed myself up from the floor. "Uh, Shark."

"Yeah."

"You got a bucket on board?"

One could only hold it so long. That I'd learned too from my Grandma Murphy who always claimed women should have a mantra: Never pass a john without going in.

10

We returned to the canal behind Shark's house by four p.m. As we motored in, Shark gave a sharp whistle. A great blue flew out of nowhere and landed on the console. "This is Mick. Me and Nell's pet." He chuckled, holding out a chum. "He's always hungry. Here you go, Mick. Take it. Go on."

Mick snatched the bait out of Shark's hand and in one gulp it was gone. Shark held out another. Gone.

This was the first time I realized that a wild bird could be trained to come at a signal. I knew about homing pigeons of course and parrots being carried about on someone's arm, but a bird in the wild hopping onboard from a whistle? Super cool, if you asked me. Once the bird was full, it flew to the bow and became our masthead. Why it took me this long not to think about the great blue at Tomas's trailer I couldn't explain. But once the light bulb went on, I took advantage of the light.

"Was this Tomas's pet too?"

"Tomas and Mick? Nah."

"Someone told me that Tomas had a thing for great blues."

"Who doesn't? They're incredible birds. Smart and loyal."

Fascinated, I continued to watch Shark feed his pet. I needed to find out if the great blue inside Tomas's trailer was merely a wild bird walking in an open door or was possibly owned by the murderer. I couldn't shake the notion that the bird was an important clue, but Shark didn't have any further enlightening information, so I filed the idea.

I needed to investigate Tomas's college life, broaden his profile. Many people reinvented themselves when they left the small community they were raised in. I wondered if Tomas had done this. Having a Mexican mother and a Caucasian father wouldn't cause any eyes to bat at a college in Cambridge, but I wondered if that were the same at a university in Florida.

I hopped off the boat. I had one hour before I was to meet Jay Mann, the sculptor who had settled in Matlacha to follow his dream of creating from clay. This hefty, shaved-head man who I first had mistaken as a skinhead wanted to take me to an early dinner. Although hesitant, I had accepted. Jay was innocent enough. There was no reason to totally avoid him. Besides, I was taking off right after I nabbed a killer.

"Watch your back," Shark said as I slid behind my steering wheel.

When I arrived at my inn room, I placed my hat on Gar's head and showered. Jay had suggested we go to the Tarpon Lodge. We could walk around first, climb a Calusa shell mound and then eat. While I was brushing my hair, he knocked on the door and I smiled at myself in the mirror. It was silly, I knew, but I felt like a high school teen going out on my first date, I was that nervous.

I put down my brush, patted Gar's head for luck and went to the door.

Jay, looking like an angelfish, was dressed in sandals, white chinos, and a blue and yellow silk shirt. He was holding a bouquet of mixed flowers in one hand and a box of what I was sure was candy from the fudge shop in the other. His grin was sheepish. "I couldn't decide which you'd like best, so I brought both."

I welcomed him into the room and went to find a vase. "They're beautiful. So thoughtful. Thanks." I arranged the flowers and set the vase on the nightstand by Gar.

"Open the box."

"Chocolates? Dark chocolate?"

His expression darkened. "But Chris said . . ."

I laughed. "I'm sorry. I was teasing. If you told Chris who you were giving them to, I'm sure it's peanut butter fudge. Thanks."

His face reddened.

Oh, dear. We were truly acting like teenagers. How embarrassing. What would Grandma Murphy think? She'd love it. Absolutely love it. The smile on her wrinkle-free face would bloom and light up the sky like sunrise after an overcast day.

I took Jay's arm and guided him toward the open door. As we stepped out onto the dock, a pelican, Will's totem, flew overhead. I hesitated.

"Make you sad?"

It's time to move on, Jessie. You can't mourn forever. Grandma's voice in my head was as clear as the blue of a cloudless sky and fluttered like the tinkling of Tinkerbell's wisdom. Grandma's voice was always a surprise to people. With her robust figure and her tall stature, people expected her words to boom. Boom is not what they did.

I blinked and returned my attention to Jay. "A bit sad, yes, but I'm okay." Tilting my head toward him I squeezed his arm and we strolled down the dock, passing the Adirondack chairs and two men fishing.

On the ride to Pineland where the 1926 Tarpon Lodge had been built, I caught a glimpse of a wild boar as Jay talked about the conference he was planning to attend this summer. Occasionally, I gazed at my reflection in the window glass. The woman looking back appeared pensive, guarded—not ready. I lowered my eyes.

The parking lot was full so Jay parked at the nearby Randall Research Center, a permanent facility dedicated to learning and teaching the archaeology, history, and ecology of the once powerful Calusa people of Southwest Florida. For centuries the Calusa accumulated huge shell mounds, engineered canals, and sustained tens of thousands of people from the fish and shellfish found in the rich estuaries. Will and I had visited the site many times. He assured me the area was haunted by Calusa ghosts. I never argued about it. When we first met I told him about my childhood ghost friends and he said this was one of many things we had in common.

No one was about. I stepped out of the car. The clack clack clack of a train's wheels made me frown. A train? Out here? In the next second, I was immediately struck by a powerful gust of wind. "Hey!" My skirt whirled high. I struggled to flatten it. My hair whipped around my face, blinding me. Leaves snapped at my bare legs. A twig smacked my upper arm. "Ouch!"

Jay ran around the car. "What the . . . !" He grabbed for me as I lost my balance. The second his hand encircled my arm, the wind died down. Disappeared. Wasn't there at all. It was like the wind hadn't happened. The sky was as calm as a baby at rest.

Mystified, I caught my breath. Jay pulled me to him and looked every which way. I did the same. Not one palm frond swayed. Not one flower was bent or broken.

"If I hadn't seen that, I wouldn't believe it," he said.

I tried to make a joke about it, but the truth was, the incident scared me. So shoot me if I'm superstitious. But it was like some otherworldly spirit was trying to frighten us away. I couldn't help but think of what Shark had said: There's less evil spirits on the water than on land. Now if "it"—the visitor—had been a human, I wouldn't have budged. No way. I would have stood my ground like Custer at his Last Stand. As it was, I told Jay I wanted to return to my room. My stomach was upset. I didn't think food would settle well.

A half hour later I was curled up with Gar on top of my comforter trying to convince myself that Will hadn't made a visit with the purpose of keeping Jay and I apart and that I and/or Tomas's family weren't in danger of being the murderer's next victims.

Being Irish can have its drawbacks.

11

After my morning exercise and breakfast, I looked up Gulf Coast University's phone number and gave them a call. They referred me to Tomas's adviser.

If the adviser knew nothing, she could at least direct me to Tomas's professors. Then I'd contact his roommates and friends. If Shark was right that something had caused an emotional or intellectual crisis at the university, someone on campus should have information.

The adviser could see me at four thirty. I hung up and with mental fingers crossed, made another call. The phone rang three times. On the fourth, I recognized Caitlin's voice. I was in luck.

"Hey, Caitlin, this is Jessie Murphy. Is there a time we could meet and talk?"

"I really don't have anything to say to you."

"Listen, I have a few questions, that's all. Tomas's mom asked me to ask them. I'm just trying to help her out. It won't take long. I'm happy to come up to Sarasota."

After a long pause during which I feared she'd hang up, I heard, "Well, there's this pizza place on 41, Café Amalfi. It's quiet."

"Perfect. How about lunch? I haven't had pizza for ages." Well, not since yesterday anyway.

"Sure. I'll meet you at twelve thirty. Do you have a GPS?"

I assured her I did. It was ten thirty. I had plenty of time to get there, talk to her and still get to Florida Gulf Coast U. "Great! See you there."

I drove directly to the pizza house. Caitlin sat at a table farthest from the door. Her head was partially hidden behind an open book.

"Studying?" I asked, pulling out a chair and sitting. The place smelled of baking crust and French fries.

Caitlin closed the hardback and set it on the table near a holder containing condiments. She met my eyes for a brief second, and then studied the jacket cover of the chemistry textbook. Not having the type of brain to do well in science courses beyond my freshman year in college, I was impressed. "Thanks for seeing me," I said, "especially on such short notice."

She nodded.

I placed my handbag on the seat beside me. "What's your major?"

"Pre-med," she mumbled.

"Whoa! Super cool. Science was never my bag. You know what you plan to specialize in?"

"Internal medicine."

This gal needed a refresher course in successful small talk more than me. I was glad when the waitress showed up, took our drink order and left menus. We agreed to share a small mushroom and anchovy pizza. I saw it as a sign we were making communication progress. "Cheese sticks?" I asked. She shrugged.

I interlocked my fingers and leaned forward. Caitlin's rounded shoulders, bent head and downcast eyes defined shyness or poor self-esteem. I wondered how she and Tomas had met.

I cleared my throat. "I thought I'd see you and your family at the funeral."

Caitlin stared at a bad painting of an Italian villa that hung on the wall. "We planned to come, but that morning my

75

grandfather had a stroke. We spent the day in the hospital. It was dreadful in the emergency room. All those sick people. No one seemed to be helping any of them. I hope . . ." The sentence drifted away.

"I'm sorry. How's your grandfather doing?"

"He'll be okay." She rubbed her fingers over her forehead.

I felt sorry for her. I never knew my grandfathers. They'd died before I was born. My dad's mom had died when I was one. But Grandma Murphy lived next door to our house since I was two. Although I knew she wouldn't live forever, thinking of her as not part of my life wasn't easy. "I won't keep you long. As I said, if it weren't for his mother and her need to get answers, I wouldn't be bothering you at all. Tomas never told me how you two met."

"In anatomy class. We were lab partners." Her eyes locked on her book.

"His mom was told that something occurred that made Tomas change. Do you have any idea what that was?"

She shook her head. "I'd ask his roommate, Ty about that."

"Ty Chambers?"

Caitlin nodded.

"But you agree that he changed?"

She shifted in the chair. The pizza arrived. We ate a full piece before she answered. Apparently, eating together made her more comfortable with me, because she began talking before I had to ask another question.

"Tomas *did* change. That's why he broke up with me. He never told me what happened. I came back from a weekend with my folks and he refused to see me. I called and called. Left voice mails. But he never called back. I was devastated. Then one day I saw him on campus walking with another female student. When he saw me, he turned away. I figured he'd lost interest in me."

I wiped my mouth with the paper napkin. "When did this happen?"

"About two weeks after class started this semester."

"But your brother said that while you were away on spring break with your parents that he called you repeatedly."

"I know. That was a surprise. I didn't know anything about it until Robert told you. Robert said he didn't leave any voicemails and he never emailed me or texted me either."

"And your dad said he loved Tomas."

Caitlin's head dipped toward her pizza plate. "I never told my family about our breakup. My parent's biggest worry was that I'd never find a man. I didn't date in high school. I was one of the class nerds. I just let them think I still had a boyfriend. There didn't seem to be any harm in that."

"No, of course there wasn't." I made a motion with my hand for the bill. "Would you give me Tomas's roommate's name and perhaps any other friends' names? Maybe they can give Mariana some information that will help her get over this tragic loss. "

Caitlin reached into her breast pocket and handed me a folded piece of paper. "Here, I made a list. I figured you'd want one." She rubbed her forehead again and for the first time looked me directly in the eye. "Please find out the truth about Tomas's death." Her voice caught. She tilted her head toward the book.

"I'm sure you read that cocaine was found in Tomas's trailer?"

Her eyes widened. "He would never take drugs. No way. But," she said hesitantly, "I can only speak for when I was with him, I suppose."

I patted her hand. "I'll do the best I can. This list should help. Oh, one thing." I tapped on the skeleton photo and showed it to her. "Does this mean anything to you?"

She looked at the photo for the longest time. So long that I was positive it had a significance that I was sure to learn. Instead, she finally shook her head and said it meant nothing, nothing at all to her.

I wondered.

When I left, she was still sitting at the table, hugging the book to her chest.

I tried to make sense of what I'd learned as I walked to my car. So Tomas had broken up with Caitlin. Not vice versa. And Shark was right. Something had happened to Tomas, something that made him turn away from his shy girlfriend. I didn't think he'd learned that Caitlin was two-timing him. She wasn't that type. Perhaps her brother had scared him off. That seemed unlikely, especially if it were true that Tomas was trying to contact her during spring break.

I looked at the list she had given me: Ty Chambers, Dr. Sarah Peters, and Dr. David Napier.

Apparently Tomas had very few friends, anyway, that Caitlin knew.

I needed to talk to Brother Robert, but first to the people at Florida Gulf Coast U.

12

Dr. Sarah Peters had black hair and hazel eyes set in a wide, pleasant face. Her front teeth had a gap and her smile was engaging. She wore a blue silk blouse and a large red and black necklace with a medallion in the shape of an owl—matching earrings. I pulled off my cap and regretted my jeans and T-shirt. A scent of Lady Gaga perfume permeated the room.

The window behind the adviser's desk provided a panoramic view of a lake complete with ibis, mallards, and one great blue heron. I wondered how many students appreciated this paradise.

The woman stood and we shook hands. "How may I help you?"

"As I told you," I said, "I'm here to talk to you about Tomas Moore. His mom is in a terrible state. I'm a family friend. She asked me to find out about his life on campus. She seems to think it will help her grieving process. I am aware that there are things you can't tell me, what with you being his adviser and all, but anything would be of help to Tomas's mother. She's so distraught."

A shadow crossed over Dr. Peters` face. "Well, since he's dead, well, I'll do the best I can to help. However, in a situation like this we are legally bound to give out no information about a student unless the request is from the police department." She leaned forward. Her complexion darkened. The large medallion scraped the desk top.

With her bright color selection of clothes and the over-sized necklace and matching earrings, it occurred to me that Dr. Peters might be Latino or Native American.

"Professors cannot discuss our students or their lives on campus." She rested her arms on the desk and caught me looking at her wedding ring. "I've been married for six years. My husband is in Afghanistan. He's a lieutenant in the army." She looked at the ring. "With all the school shootings it's almost too scary to teach. He wants me to quit," she mumbled, then looked at me quickly and cleared her throat.

I was shocked at her sudden information dump. Sounded like someone who needed to validate herself. But, why?

Her index finger tapped on her desk calendar. She looked at everything in the room but me.

Nervous? Of me asking questions about Tomas? What was going on?

"Tomas's mom wondered if he had some kind of personal crisis while he was here. Do you know anything about that?"

She studied my face briefly while her fingernail continued to click, making the sound of a distant woodpecker. "The truth is, I didn't see Tomas that often. Basically, only to help him choose his classes. The last time he was in was at the end of his first semester when he signed up for spring courses."

"He didn't come in this semester?"

She shook her head. "He didn't. Usually students do. But he didn't. Many like to drop in and talk. I guess it makes them feel connected to someone other than their professors and roommates and such, but Tomas wasn't that type. He was pretty independent. I do remember that he said he was the son of a crabbing family from Pine Island."

"So he told you that. In what light?"

She frowned and her fingers quivered ever so slightly. "I'm not sure what you mean."

"I mean, why did that conversation come up? That is, if telling me doesn't break some rule of confidentiality."

Her shoulders relaxed. "Oh, I see. I'd told him my husband was from a Charlotte Harbor fishing family. He asked me if the cops treated the fishermen up there like they did the Pine Island crabbers, especially the two families with Mexican blood. I asked him what he meant. 'Like robbers and thieves and rapists,' he said. 'My dad thinks the newbie cops get special training in how to handle us'."

"So Tomas was bitter about how his family was treated?"

She leaned back against her leather chair.

If I were to describe her, I would say this was a woman who had felt threatened, but now felt in control. I was fascinated.

"Well, funny enough, he wasn't. He told me this as if it were a joke. He said once the new cops got to know them their opinion changed, which I am sure is true." She smiled, leaned forward, and folded her arms on her desk. "Tomas didn't seem like the bitter type. But as I said, I didn't talk to him enough to know him that well."

She glanced at her wall clock. "You should talk to his professors." She looked at her watch. "Actually, you may be able to catch his sociology professor, David Napier. His class meets this next hour. Oh, but Ms. Murphy . . ."

"Yes."

"You didn't get any helpful information from me; if you claim you did, I'll deny it."

Smart woman. Covering her educated butt.

I thanked her and left before I realized I had forgotten to show her the skeleton (I'd remedy that later) or ask for directions to the sociology department. The walkways teemed with students, laughing and chatting. A young man with sandy-colored hair in baggy shorts and a flowered shirt strolled toward me. I stopped him and asked if he knew where Lincoln Hall was located. He pointed to a building down another path. I thanked him and hurried in that direction.

Napier was standing behind a desk, rifling through a stack of papers. He wore a white, long-sleeved shirt, a striped tie, and khaki pants. Two students sat in the back of the room with their heads together. Others pushed around me as they took their seats. I headed for the desk, introduced myself and was met by a pair of solemn, alert eyes. Glancing at the room, Napier motioned toward the door and I followed him into the hall. We went to the far wall.

"What can I do for you?" he asked.

I told him about my fake purpose for being on campus. He nodded and said I should meet him in his office after class. I went to the cafeteria. I would telephone Tomas's roommate from there and hopefully be able to see him this evening.

My monkey ringtone laughed. Jay. I bit down on my lip. He wanted to know if I could meet him for lunch the next day. Starting a relationship? Now, when I was leaving the islands? Be sensible, I told myself. Stay clear of him. Besides, there was that scary incident near the Calusa mounds. I begged off.

The cafeteria was expansive, brightened by the sun's rays streaming in through the ceiling to floor windows. I took my place in line and picked up a tray. Not a fan of cafeteria food, I decided yogurt and fruit would be a sound snack choice. I reached for a plastic bowl of melon and strawberries covered in clear plastic wrap.

"Excuse me."

I looked over my shoulder.

"Are you the person asking about Tomas Moore?"

"I am."

"I was Tomas's roommate. I think we met briefly at his funeral."

The roommate finding me? How interesting.

I paid for my food and headed for the young man who waited for me near a potted palm. He was about twenty, had curly brown hair, wore tortoise-rimmed glasses, and was a nerd by anyone's standards. He tugged at his earlobe as I sat.

I extended my hand. "Jessie Murphy," I said.

"Ty Chambers," he offered, shaking my hand.

"How did you find out I was on campus? I had planned to call you while I ate."

"Dr. Peters texted me."

I concentrated on opening my carton of yogurt. Had I mentioned wanting to talk to Tomas's roommate with the adviser? I didn't think so. I peeled off the foil lid and picked up my plastic spoon. "How thoughtful of her," I said. "It must be difficult for you having lost your friend."

His eyes were flat gun-metal gray. He straightened his glasses by putting his pointer finger on the crossbar between the lenses. "We weren't actually friends," he said. "Just roommates."

"Is Dr. Peters your adviser too?"

"Yeah."

I readjusted myself in my chair and then addressed his comment about his relationship with Tomas. "Not much in common?"

"Nothing, in fact."

"I see." I took another bite. "So, what's your major?" I studied him under the brim of my cap. He looked over his shoulder and rubbed the fingers of his right hand with his left. The guy was tense; must be a virus rampant on campus. At my question, he settled back into his chair.

"English."

"And Tomas's major was?"

"Engineering."

I wiped my mouth. "You ever party together?"

"Tomas wasn't the partying type."

"And you are?"

That elicited a smile. "Only on weekends."

I watched him while I ate.

"What was your impression of Tomas?"

"He was all right. Kind of quiet. Studied a lot. Secretive."

"Secretive?"

"You know how most people talk about their folks and siblings? Well, Tomas never said anything about his. We used to wonder what all the hush-hush was all about."

"We? Is there another roommate?" I popped a delicious cardboard tasty strawberry slice into my mouth. Got to love cafeteria food.

"Nah. My fraternity brothers. At first, I thought I might ask Tomas to pledge, but, well, since he was so secretive and all, I didn't bother." He straightened in his chair. "Phi Delta Theta was the first fraternity on campus. It's a *select* house."

Oh, my. Such arrogance. I let it go. I couldn't see that a sarcastic remark would further my cause. "Did you notice any change in Tomas's personality the last few months?"

He touched his glasses. "Not really."

"He just seemed the same old Tomas?"

"Well, he wasn't too pleased about his girlfriend situation."

"How so?"

"He said he had broken up with her and that her brother didn't want him around. He wouldn't put her through any conflict."

"That was thoughtful of Tomas, wouldn't you say?"

Ty's eyebrows arched. "I wouldn't let a bro scare me away, not if I cared for the girl. Tomas was a wimp." Then apparently remembering Tomas was dead, he added, "Sorry. I shouldn't of said that. A bummer, if you ask me. I met his girlfriend once. She's one of those mousy, studious types, if you know what I mean. I don't know what he saw in her."

Was he talking about the same young woman? The beautiful Caitlin Howard?"

"You're talking about Caitlin Howard?"

"Sure."

"His folks were wondering if Tomas had any enemies on campus. Get into any fights? Make anyone mad? Suddenly start acting different?"

"Not that I know of," he said, fiddling with a pen he'd taken out of his pocket. "And he seemed the same quiet guy to me, except for the girlfriend gig, of course."

"Were you surprised to learn Tomas took drugs?"

He looked at me sharply. "Absolutely."

"No hint at all that he used them?"

Ty rolled the pen between his palms. "I had no idea. He certainly never smoked weed or did hard drugs around me.

84

He'd have known I would turn him in. My folks would stop paying my tuition if they thought I had any contact with anyone taking drugs. Tomas knew that."

Oh sure, buddy. I believe you.

I showed him the skeleton photo and told him where I got it.

"Hah, I knew it. Tomas was involved in voodoo stuff."

"Voodoo stuff?"

He looked at me squarely. "Isn't that what you think?"

I assured him I was keeping an open mind and then turned the talk away from Tomas and finished my snack. Picking up my handbag, I glanced at the wall clock and thanked Ty for his help. I stood and we exchanged cell phone numbers in case either of us remembered a detail that might be important. I excused myself. At the exit I looked over my shoulder. Ty was talking on his cell.

I made a mental note to do a background check on Ty Chambers and Dr. Sarah Peters. They were certainly now on my suspect list. Something didn't add up. Peters was far too nervous talking to me about Tomas; and Chambers, unless my hunch proved wrong, was lying about his not using drugs. It was also very odd that the adviser had contacted the roommate and alerted him I was on campus.

When I strolled into Napier's office, he was sliding a paperback into a floor to ceiling shelf stuffed with other books. He turned as I entered.

"Ah, Ms. Murphy, glad you found me." He had loosened his tie and rolled up his sleeves. His air was friendly.

Almost every available spot was occupied by books and typing paper. He walked to a chair, picked up two volumes and set them on the floor. "Here, take a seat. Excuse the mess. I'm in the midst of a research project."

"I thought most people used the net," I said, sitting. "So many books."

He chuckled. "I'm an old-fashioned guy," he said. "I like the feel of a book in my hand. Besides, much of my research hasn't been put on the net yet." He sat. His desk faced the wall.

The visitor chair looked toward the left side of his desk. He placed his arms on his swivel chair and turned it to me. His office smelled of musty paper and yellowed hardbacks. His carpet was coffee stained. A large computer monitor was surrounded by piles of what looked like a manuscript in progress. Three diplomas were framed in black on the wall. He'd received his Ph.D. from Penn State, Masters from Southern Illinois.

He interrupted my study of his credentials by asking why I had come to see him.

After I established that I was a family friend trying to get some information to help the Moores find closure, he tilted his head, his expression patient and composed. "Tomas Moore was only a student of mine for one course. I really didn't know him all that well," he said. "I am, as you can imagine, saddened by his death and willing to help his parents through their grieving process in any way I can. But anything I tell you will have to remain between you and me. I'm not sure what the legal ramifications are about giving information out about a student after they've passed and I don't want my reputation tarnished."

"Of course. Any information you give me will never be connected to your name. You can trust me on that."

He studied me for quite some time, then leaned back in his chair. "Okay, I'll take your word on that. Ask away."

"What was your impression of him?"

"Well, he was a serious student. He did well on exams and wrote thoughtful papers." He looked away and then back again. "If I remember right, and I think I do, he would have had one of the top grades in the course, but he missed the last two pop quizzes."

"Did he have an excuse for missing the classes?"

"He never said and I never asked. Students miss class all the time. I don't keep attendance."

"He never asked to make them up?"

Dr. Napier shook his head. "Not that I recall."

"In your experience dealing with students, is it the norm for top students to not try to maintain their grades?"

"There's nothing consistent about being a college student."

Disappointed, I looked around the room. "What's your research about?"

Napier's blue eyes brightened. "I'm putting together a historic account of the men who were arrested in the drug raids in Everglade City during the 80s."

I leaned forward. "Really? That must be fascinating?"

"Yes, it is. Did you know eventually over three hundred were arrested and over half of the fishing boats were seized? Lifestyles were devastated. Families were torn apart. Everglades City was a hotbed of drug activity for years. I've become obsessed with the research, I'm afraid. In fact, the class Tomas was taking was designed around the project. Students love the course. Popular culture is in right now with students. In fact, I'll teach it again next fall."

"Did he ever discuss aspects of the subject with you?"

"He did. The class was in the fourth or fifth week and he made an appointment to see me. He asked specific questions about those arrested and inquired about how he could get further information. I remember he said he was thankful there was no drug running activity on Pine Island. If I recall correctly he said it would be like having a Category Five Hurricane hit the island if any such activity was discovered. Him being a crabber's son, I understood his concern."

"You must have been quite surprised to read cocaine was found at the murder scene."

"I'm afraid nothing surprises me much anymore."

"You wouldn't have an extra syllabus around?"

He swiveled and rifled through papers on his desk, mumbling to himself. "Ah, hah, here we are." He held up three pages stapled together. "If you want to get the books on the reading list, you'll have to find them off campus. I've been told they are sold out as soon as the bookstore orders them. The topic is quite popular."

I skimmed the titles. "Many of these books concern crabbers."

Was it possible that was what Tomas and the people of the islands feared most, that there was drug activity in the area and their livelihoods would be affected? After all, cocaine was found. Where did he get it? Or had it been planted?

"Oh, yes. Oh, yes, indeed." He made a tower with his fingers. "If you haven't read anything about this portion of Florida's history, you're in for a treat. It's quite amazing."

Someone knocked. Napier sat up straighter. "I'm sorry. I have conferences scheduled with students for the rest of the day. I'd be happy to talk to you another time."

Assuring him I would call him, I excused myself and walked toward the office door. I turned. "Oh, just in case you think of something else, let me leave my phone number." I scribbled on the back of a Publix receipt and put it on his desk. "And one more thing, did Ty Chambers take that class?"

"Yes, I believe he did."

As I stepped into the hallway, I asked myself again why Dr. Peters had telephoned Ty Chambers. I decided to stop into her office to thank her. Pulling out my cell phone, I saw that I had a voicemail from Jay. I bit down on my lower lip and re-pocketed the phone. I was also reminded that I had forgotten to ask both the doctors about the skeleton doll. I would start with Dr. Peters and return to Napier after.

The campus was quiet. Even the birds had found somewhere else to roost. A lavender, pink, and golden sunset made the lawn gleam. I stepped into Lutgert Hall.

Two loud pops in succession made my foot freeze in midair. I knew gunfire when I heard it. In the past year, I'd decided to get a firearm and monthly went to a firing range to practice. A scream brought goose bumps to my flesh. I dashed down the corridor. A man and a woman stood in an open doorway.

The man had his arm around the sobbing woman's shoulder and a cell phone in his other hand. "Yes, yes! There's been a shooting!" He gave the location.

Shattered glass covered the carpet. Two men knelt over the body. The prone woman's dark-skinned arm was extended beyond the desk. I saw her wedding ring and my heart sank.

13

I hung around campus long enough to see Dr. Peters` body rolled out on a stretcher and to answer the cop's questions. A little voice niggled at me that perhaps, just perhaps, there was a connection with my investigation and this death. I filed the thought for later examination.

As I bypassed the crowd, I saw Tomas's roommate talking to another male student. I pulled out my cell and took his picture and then returned to my car.

This evening I would call Robert Howard, Caitlin's brother. According to Deputy Tobin Peterson, Robert had an angry conversation with Tomas the night he died. I wanted to know what it had been about.

I listened to Jay's voicemail. He wanted to meet me for dinner. I sighed and closed the phone. Didn't he get it? I can't. I just can't.

More than glad to see Gar waiting for me in my room, I settled my cap on his head, went to the bathroom and took a long shower. Normally, I don't take two showers in a day—but I wanted to wash away any hint of death still clinging to me. It would be months before I could erase the image of Dr. Peters` friendly face from my mind. And with her husband in Afghanistan. How dreadful. The fact she had acted a bit cagey to me nagged at my gray cells as well.

As I let water cleanse my body, I thought about what I had learned on campus: Tomas, a dedicated, goal-oriented student, had missed some quizzes, which had affected his grade, but he hadn't asked to make them up. What made him miss them? He'd taken a course about the history of drugs in the Everglades that apparently had been of high interest to him. A connection?

I turned off the faucet, pushed open the glass door, and grabbed a towel. The porcelain towel bar careened to the tile floor, snapping in two. Dang. The phone rang. I left the damaged bar where it was, rubbed my dripping hair, then wrapped the towel around me. By the time my monkey ring tone was through laughing the phone went dead. I picked it up. No voicemail. I checked "Recent Calls" and saw a number I didn't recognize. I clicked on it.

"Hello, this is Jessie Murphy," I said. "Sorry I missed your call."

"Jessie, this is Caitlin. I was wondering if we could talk again." Her voice was low—not quite a whisper but close.

I assured her that we could. We set a place and time— Matlacha. A restaurant not far from the inn. Eight p.m. When I hit "End Call" I made sure to save Caitlin's number.

If I ran into Jay, I'd just tell him I hadn't gotten his voicemail.

The parking lot was more than packed. I had to make a U-turn in order to find a space in front of an eight-foot metal fence facing a canal. For a shy woman to pick such a crowded restaurant was interesting to say the least. As my flip flops crunched on gravel, I wondered if Caitlin was the type of woman to choose a meeting place with purpose. Remembering that she was quite intelligent, I decided she was.

Stepping inside, I nodded at two young hostesses, telling them I was meeting someone. They smiled as I passed on. Caitlin was sitting in the first booth. The noise level was deafening. Knowing she had a soft voice, I hoped she'd brought a microphone.

The room held probably fifty people or more. The ceiling was yellowed from previous, now banned, cigarette smoke. Every time the back door opened, strains of live music assaulted us. The place smelled like garlic and onions.

It was eight o'clock sharp. I ordered a Guinness. Caitlin was sipping a dull pink liquid. Perhaps lemonade. I doubted it contained alcohol. I couldn't help but think of Ty's description of her. Mousy? Really? She was lovely.

"Nice to see you again," I said, resting my arms on the table's edge.

She greeted me with a sad smile—a tiny one. Her eyelids flickered. She seemed so lost.

"You must be surprised," she said, "me calling you and all."

Her eyes were hazel and her thick lashes free of mascara. Waterford-crystal skin. Loose-fitting pale blue shirt. No jewelry. Manicured nails painted with tiny buttercups—artfully—not garish like some I'd seen. Do mousy young women paint their nails?

I smiled. "Lovely artwork on your nails."

She dropped her hands into her lap. "My mom's idea," she mumbled.

Tomas must have angst for days before dropping this lovely child-woman. She looked hauntingly like the frail, lifeless body that John Everett Millais painted of Shakespeare's Ophelia as she lay amongst lily pads.

"You have something to tell me?

She nodded again. "Yes. It's something, that I . . . that I lied about. Well . . ." Her words faded away.

"And you couldn't tell me whatever it is over the phone?"

She looked at me with a shocked expression. I felt like I had slapped her face. "Oh, no, Rob . . ." Another long pause.

Giving her time, I sipped my Guinness. With what I hoped was a soothing voice I said, "I'm listening."

"What I said before was a lie." She lowered her head.

Our table was lit with stifled light. I can take "stifle" only so long. I leaned across the table. The people in the booth behind exploded in laughter. "Caitlin, Robert isn't here. Please tell me what you need to say. If you say it quickly . . . well, it will be out. You can trust me. I hope you know that."

Caitlin, too, stretched her upper body across the rough wooden table, our heads a mere six inches apart. Her words were coated in urgency. "My brother didn't like Tomas. My brother doesn't like any boy who might like me. My brother is *more than* protective." Her last sentence came out as an ominous whisper, moist eyes were the size of cotton balls. She looked hunted, fearful and slunk back against the booth. Her shoulders rounded and her head lowered.

Overprotective. I wasn't surprised.

What was only seconds, but seemed like hours, later, I spoke. "It can be hard to have an overprotective brother."

Her fingers interlocked. "It's more than that."

I frowned. More than that? I blanched at my next conclusion. "You aren't saying that your brother abuses you?"

Caitlin nodded. "Sexually." The word came out as a whisper as tears streamed down her face. She did nothing to hide them.

She continued in such a soft voice, I had to lean closer. "I'm sorry. What did you say?"

"I told Tomas."

Her words were too incredible to believe. "You told Tomas that you were being sexually abused by your brother and he broke up with you?"

No way. This didn't fit the profile of the caring Tomas I had constructed.

"I . . . I . . . I'm not sure he broke up with me. He wouldn't talk about it, not after that night, but . . ."

"But when you told him, you didn't talk? Surely you talked. Tomas had to have been upset."

"Oh, yes. He was, but not with me. He swore he would take care of Robert. That I wasn't to worry about him. Robert would never again bother me."

"When did this happen?"

"I told him the night before my parents and I left for spring break."

"Has Robert bothered you since then?"

She cringed. "Last night he . . . he . . ." Her chin sunk against her chest.

My heart felt like it had been buried under six feet of dirt. "Oh, Caitlin, you must tell the police. He must be stopped."

"But, I've told you."

Stunned, I stared at her. Yes, she had told me. A complete stranger. She had told me. I reached for her hand. I had once not answered a similar call for help by a college friend. She had killed herself. I would not let that happen again. "Yes, you have. And we'll do something about it. Together. Tonight."

Her eyes did not leave mine.

"We must go to the police. You must tell them what you've told me. What Robert has been doing to you must be stopped for good. Right?"

Caitlin's fingers tightened, but she did not pull back. "O . . . kay."

I motioned for the check. "Let's go."

"Go where?"

"Caitlin, have you been listening to me? We are going to the sheriff's office tonight."

"Tonight? Like now? What about my parents?" Her face was a mask of terror.

"Why do you think you never confided in them?"

Caitlin's face paled. Her lower lip quivered.

"You came to me for a reason. You can trust me with this. Leave your car here. We'll drive together. Come on."

I paid the bill and directed Caitlin to walk in front of me. She pushed open the door. Like tiny fish hooks, the hot breeze pricked our skin.

"Damn!" I said, hesitating.

"What?" Caitlin asked.

"It just occurred to me that the sheriff may not be working tonight. I'd like her to hear this firsthand." I gazed steadily at

Caitlin. Then: "You can stay with me. I have a sofa bed. We'll go to the sheriff in the morning. You can call your folks and tell them you're staying at a friend's. Okay?"

"Why don't I just go home?"

"Where Robert lives?"

She stumbled.

I steadied her. "No. You're better off with me. We'll get through this together."

A cloud passed over the man in the moon.

We drove our own cars to the Bridgewater Inn, Caitlin in the lead.

Inside the efficiency, after introducing her to Gar and accepting the "a-gargoyle-as-a-friend-really" look, Caitlin told me she was exhausted and wanted to go right to bed. We pulled out the sleep sofa. She brushed her teeth—seemed she always kept an extra toothbrush with her—and climbed under the sheets. By the time I came out of the bathroom, perhaps ten minutes later, she was lightly snoring. I would have been amazed, but I knew someone else who had this incredible ability to fall asleep when she felt as if she were in a safe place. She, too, had been sexually abused by a once trusted relative.

Not sleepy, I grabbed my sketchpad, took a Guinness, turned off the lamp and went outside, closing the door softly. A guy at the end of the dock was fishing. Our eyes caught and we nodded our greetings. I settled in a striped Adirondack chair. Moonlight slithered across the rippling water like a snake. Two crab trap buoys bobbed ever so slightly. I put back my head and let the hum of the waves and the acrid organic odor of the sea lull me into my creative zone. After withdrawing my pencil from my shirt pocket, I began to draw.

Sketching and drawing were *my* escapes—my release from a world rife with murder, domestic violence, theft and downright mean-spirited people. I was more than thankful I had this passion. Many I'd met didn't have one. I often found if someone didn't have at least one passion, they'd direct the energy toward need: I need to buy this. I need you to . . . for me. Even, in the extreme—I need you to take care of me. Such people's egos were hard to satisfy, and more importantly, these people didn't understand that they were needy. Solitude to them was an enemy. Solitude for someone with a creative passion was a necessity.

Grandma Murphy once told me: "To such people being needy is their passion. Watch out for them. They have a desire to swallow you whole."

I studied my drawing. Since beginning, I hadn't been totally conscious of what my hand had been doing, so I now studied my work for the first time. I looked at the fisherman, then at my sketchpad. On my page, a man with his foot on the railing was fishing. A bait bucket sat near his bare left ankle. He wore cut-off jeans and a muscle shirt. He had a shiny bald scalp. A bushy beard covered his upper chest. The face was Jay Mann's.

The man on the dock reeled in his line. I closed my sketchpad. Through the open window of my room, I heard Caitlin moan. The fisherman tied his bait bucket to a piling and slipped it into the water before taking his fishing gear inside.

A sharp noise behind me made me press my sketchpad protectively against my chest. Still sitting, I turned my upper body and stared into the eyes of Russ Beadle. I reminded myself I hadn't had Hawk do a background check on him. He may not be the killer (by now I was convinced it was Robert Howard), but I'm sure he was someone I wanted to know about so I could always be prepared. Like now.

The snake tat on Russ's bicep seemed ready to strike.

The second thing that crossed my mind was: Thank you, Grandma, for insisting that I take those karate classes. Fully alert, I pushed myself out of the low chair. "What are you doing here?" I hoped my growl was effective.

Russ, wearing a dirty white T-shirt, overalls, and white rubber boots, hesitated and withdrew a cigarette pack from his pocket. "You interested in talkin` with me?" He pulled out a lighter.

"Yeah, but I'd heard you were in Key West."

"Was. Leavin` again in a couple days. What's up?"

"You always in the habit of making visits late at night?" It was ten fifteen.

His lips curled into a smirk. "Best time to catch sisters like you at home." His eyes went to my bare legs.

Such a first class jerk. So ten fifteen wasn't late. So shoot me. Although I was convinced Tomas's killer, Robert Howard, would be arrested in the morning after Caitlin and I went to talk to the sheriff, I figured why not see what this guy knew.

I led him away from the open window. Further down the dock, I stopped and put my forearms on the railing to quell my nerves. In the distance a sailboat bobbed like a cork above a baited hook. Russ turned his back to the railing, leaned against it and faced the inn. It was an odd way to conduct an interview, but, oh well . . .

"Mariana Moore has some questions about her son's death."

"So I heard. Ask away. I'll be honest with ya. You can count on it. Mariana deserves that."

"I was told Tomas worked for you."

"Yep. Some."

"When did he start?"

"Ah, let's see. Guess he started in high school. Maybe when he was round fifteen or so."

I frowned and glanced Russ's way. "That long?"

"Yep. His folks didn't know about it. The kid said he was saving money for college." Russ flicked his cigarette into the water. "He was a real hard worker. Got snapped in the belly once by a big sucker crab, but that didn't stop him. Real tough, that one."

"Was he working for you during spring break?"

"Yep."

I turned around and faced Russ. "You know anything about him using drugs?"

"Nope. Not him."

"So you knew nothing about Tomas and hard drugs?"

97

Russ wiped the back of his hand across his grizzly chin. "Listen, woman, I'd bet my boat against that lame notion. That kid never took hard drugs in his life.

The kid needed money, but he was honest as my ex-wife. She's the honestest woman I ever knew. Not like me. I've been in prison five times. Seems it's my second home.

Anyways, the kid hears that a couple of sport fishermen was looking for someone who knew the local waters. He hooks up with them. Mind you, this is straight from his mouth. So, they go out and the two guys are sniffin` all night long." Russ looked hard at me. "You know what I mean, right?" He placed his index finger on the side of his nose and pressed.

I nodded. Cocaine.

"Tomas was fit to be hogtied, but there's nothin` he can do, so he bides his time and sticks to himself. Lots of drinkin` goin` on too. Anyways, Tomas spots a boat headin` their way. He alerts the guys, but they're already standing aft. The boat ties alongside. But Tomas won't tell me what's being transferred. Said it was best I didn't know." Russ lit another cigarette. "My guess, it was hollowed out coconuts filled with coke. It's the usual way of bringing it in." He inhaled. "Tomas knew he was in a tight situation. Nothin` to do but help. Pissed a`course and scared. Knows what it'll mean if they get caught. Prison. No more college. Shame, maybe even loss of their boat, for his folks. But he does what they say." Russ coughed. "When they get back to the dock, Tomas hops off and runs. No pay."

"Did he turn them in?"

"Get jailed himself? No way."

"Those guys must have been worried about what Tomas would say."

"Oh, yeah. And Tomas figured that and he was afraid, man."

"When did this happen?"

"Night he died. He came right to me. He was supposed to go out with me crabbing the next morning. He was a mess. I knew he'd be useless—the way his hands were shakin` and

98

all. I told him I didn't want him on my boat—that he was over-reactin`. To go talk to his pa." He looked into the distance. "Damn, wish I hadn't blown him off."

"Tomas was more likely afraid what might happen to the family business and to his folks than to his own butt. I'm sure you know about Everglades City."

"You bet we all know and you can bet no one with a brain in their head around here is having anything to do with drug trafficking. We may not be edecated, but we ain't dumb. We're keepin` our noses clean on that score."

"You don't think any locals are involved?"

"I think the smart ones are scared, not involved. They got families. They like their freedom. The feds did a wide sweep in the glades. Lots of innocent people got hurt. My uncle's family was one of them. No one wants that to happen here."

"You didn't, by chance, get the guy's names?"

"If I had, I reckon you wouldn't be able to talk to them by now."

I got his meaning. He would have beat them to unconsciousness, or worse.

"Have you told Tomas's story to the cops?"

Dumb question. And throw suspicion of drug running on his parents? No way.

"I reckon we don't need help from the likes of them. Anything else?"

I shook my head "no," but then thought of something. "Did Tomas ever talk to you about his girlfriend?"

"You mean, Cat? Sure. Sweet thing. Tomas brought her out crabbin` one time. She ain't no pansy, I can tell you that. Captains a boat like a pro."

"There's a rumor that they broke up."

"Couldn't prove it by me. Last I knew they were love bugs."

There went my theory that Beadle had started that rumor.

"Tomas ever talk about Cat's brother?"

Russ glared at a piling. His expression hardened.

"Tomas told me about that low-life. Last I knew he was planning to take Cat with him to the cops."

"Did Tomas confront the brother?"

"Don't know. All's I knows is that if Tomas wanted I'd cut off the brother's balls for him and wouldn't charge a penny."

When I showed him the skeleton doll photo he shrugged and claimed to know nothing. "But if he gave this to Gator and said not to give it to you unless somethin` happened to him like you say, you can bet he was trying to tell you somethin`. He was fearful of something evil and that doll don't look like no sweet Barbie."

How would the doll fit into drug running? What was the connection I was missing?

Beadle gave me a no-nonsense look and walked away. The sound of his boots hitting the wooden planks bounced along the water. A truck rumbled across the bridge. The sea smelled deadlier than ever. I turned and went inside. Cat's eyes were closed. But I was too worked up to sleep. I scribbled a note to Cat on a note card. I grinned. How many times had that nun tried to get me to call them index cards? Like, give me a break, sister. I told Caitlin where she could find me, picked up other cards and stuffed them in my pocket. Bert's was a short walk away. I needed to be around people. The more the better.

So Tomas went out with a couple of crooked fishermen and came in petrified and Russ knew nothing about Caitlin and Tomas's breakup, but apparently Tomas had told him about her brother. Two possibilities: Those fishermen could have gone after Tomas, or Robert could have killed him to keep him quiet. But then there was the skeleton doll.

As I approached the bar in Bert's, Jay stood and asked another customer to switch seats. Smiling, he offered me the stool.

"Did you get my message?"

"Just did. Sorry, I forgot to check my voicemails." So spank me for lying, Grandma.

100

"Your usual?"

I nodded.

He ordered and when my Guinness arrived, he said, "Come on. Let's go out back and enjoy the million-dollar view."

A table for two was vacant. We sat. I placed my hands around my glass and looked into Jay's eyes. He looked back, then reached across the table and touched my hand.

An electric current shot through me, and to my amazement, I did not pull away.

We sat like that for several seconds, and then without speaking, without finishing our drinks, he stood and hand-in-hand we weaved through the crowd.

Jay's home was two doors down—in the opposite direction of my room. We said nothing as we walked. Stars flickered overhead. Cars passed. One honked, but I hardly noticed. Instead, I inhaled the smell of Jay's aftershave, felt the strength of his fingers around mine, and pressed against his bicep.

When he walked though his gate, he asked me to wait outside while he put his dogs into the spare room. He knew I was uncomfortable around them. Standing in the courtyard I leaned over to smell the night-blooming jasmine. My chest rose and fell.

For months I'd been avoiding this, telling myself this was a passing flirtation. My attraction for Jay was more than that. I'd always known it. Jay had always known it. Now was the time. It was glorious "I am free" time. Every fragment of my body and soul tingled. "Thank you, Will, for releasing me." I smiled at the star-studded sky. "Thank you."

I turned when the door opened and took a deep breath. Jay wore a floor-length white cotton tunic, something from the Arabian Nights. With his shaven head and broad physique, he looked like my romantic image of Genghis Khan. He extended his hand.

Marveling at my action, I took it and he led me inside. The click of the door sounded like the click a tiny brass key makes in a secret diary. I felt sealed in and gloriously not guilty.

Jay led me through his studio and into a room I had never dared to look into. His queen bed was draped in mosquito netting and covered by a white comforter. Several Turkish pillows were scattered across a white sofa. A single stem from a Bird of Paradise plant jutted out of a glass vase on a wicker nightstand. A basket in one corner was filled with rolled towels. An off-white shag area rug covered the wood floor.

Jay gently released my hand and went to an old-fashioned record player. Choosing an album, he put it on and turned. "Dance?"

With the grace and east of a professional, Jay whirled me around the floor. I only stepped on his toes twice. Each time he smiled and pulled me closer.

When the music ended, Jay eased me onto the bed.

And I let him.

14

At three a.m. when I awakened fog had settled over the island and crawled in through the sliding glass door. I rubbed my eyes as a smoke-like figure seemed to form at the end of the bed. Will? I blinked then clamped my eyes shut. When I opened them again the spectra was gone. Of course it was gone. The appearance was merely proof of my artist's imagination. That's what grandma always told me when I was a child and such things happened. I looked at Jay. He was lying on his side, his right arm flung over the mattress. What had I done? What about Caitlin? What if she awakened and needed a shoulder to cry on? Guilt like spray from a waterfall washed over me. I slipped from the bed and dressed.

Halfway back to the inn, I stopped and looked through the thinning mist into the night sky. "Oh, Will."

A star shot toward the earth.

I clasped my hands over my mouth and let the tears flow.

The next morning Caitlin was in the bathroom when I opened my eyes and yawned. The sofa was no longer pulled out. The sheets were neatly folded on one tattered arm.

I rolled to the side of the bed, sat on the edge and rumpled my hair. Leaning forward, I grabbed for my gray T-shirt and walking shorts. As I pulled my sleeping shirt over my head, I yelled, "Hey, Cat." I slipped my arms through the sleeves.

Caitlin came out of the bathroom as I was pulling back my hair into a ponytail to get ready for my morning run. "Good morning. I hope you don't mind if I keep my exercise routine," I said, reaching for my socks. "There's a good place for breakfast across from the post office. I could meet you there."

She agreed, but something in her tone of voice made the hair on the back of my neck tingle. As I tied my shoelaces, I narrowed my eyes. "You okay?"

Caitlin avoided looking at me.

I stood. "Ah, come on! Don't tell me you've changed your mind?"

She took a step backward.

"Cat! Really? Come on!"

She disappeared into the bathroom.

I knew, oh how I knew, no one could make a victim go to the cops. They had to take the step. But I had to try.

I walked toward the open door. "Ah," I said, "you don't want this to continue. If you don't turn him in and you go home, well . . ."

She cut me off. "I'm not going home. I'm returning to school. I won't see him until summer . . . and this summer my parents are sending me to France. I'll leave as quickly as I can. I don't plan to see my brother ever again."

More than discouraged, I folded my arms across my chest. Should I tell her that I suspected her brother killed Tomas? Would that help her do the right thing? With no proof? I don't think so. Not smart. But... Nah. No way.

"Cat, your brother needs to pay for what he did to you."

"And what about my parents? What do you think this would do to them?"

I grimaced.

Her next words gushed out like water from a hose. "It'll kill them." She stepped into the room.

I released the breath I'd been holding and looked at her long and hard. She had not yet combed her hair. Dark circles made her eyes look hollow. She continued to stare at the

104

yellow wall in front of her as she spoke. "I'm strong. Stronger than most think. I'm capable now of staying away from Robert. I'm even capable of forgiving him eventually. Then I'll be the one with power—not him. Not any . . . any . . . more."

If only I could convince her to go to the sheriff. I straightened my shoulders. "But, what if . . ."

She looked at me sharply, stopping my sentence like a school crossing guard. Her voice held edge. "He won't." She passed without touching me.

Dumbstruck, I remained rooted to the floor. When the door opened and sealed with a soft click, I sat—not standing for several minutes. She was gone. I'd failed.

Asking Gar to guard the room, I slipped through the door. Last year, I'd been vandalized in this same inn. With three framed paintings bagged and ready for my trip north, I sure didn't want that to happen again. I'd signed a contract with an art gallery owner in Cambridge for two of the paintings. Another was going to a juried show in Roxbury. Luckily, the show didn't begin for another month, so prolonging delivery wasn't critical. As a safeguard, I put the paintings in the closet and covered them with a sheet.

One, two times around the park. Faster. Faster. Pumping my arms, sweat pouring down my face, I slowed. Enough. Enough. It was all too much at times. Easier just to push it to the back of my mind. Two more laps around the park and I'd be done.

It was a quiet morning. A woman in a pickup was backing up a boat at the public ramp. A man stood near the water's edge guiding her. Another woman in a straw hat sat at a picnic table facing the pass, writing. Our eyes caught. She turned her head. I swung my arms high. "Hey!"

Jay, legs spread, arms extended, stood directly in my path. Unable to stop my forward motion, I stumbled into him, knocking him off balance. Laughing, he grabbed my forearms as I clutched at his shoulders. Two cattle egrets shot from tree to tree. Jay pulled me close, but I pushed away.

"Jay, last night was . . . but . . ."

"But what?"

I lowered my chin and looked at him under the bill of my cap. How did you explain to a man that you were in love with a guy who no longer lived?

He bent forward and whispered, "Surely, it was great for you too."

"Jay, please. I have *work* to do."

"Tonight then? Supper at Bert's? Eight-ish?"

I didn't say yes. I didn't say no. I merely powerwalked away—all the while feeling the push of a ghostly voice saying, "Walk faster."

I made it back to my room in record time and immediately dropped my cap onto Gar's head, stripped, went into the bathroom and took a shower, steeling myself from the constant onslaught of the water.

Wrapped in a towel, I sat on the edge of the bed and picked up a stack of note cards:

Card one: Robert Howard—No. 1 suspect. Motive: Tomas may have threatened him with arrest for incest. Seen arguing with him by Tobin Peterson.

Card two: Find out the names of the fishermen that Tomas went out with. Motive: Drug dealers could have feared Tomas would turn them in.

Card three: Was Dr. Peters' murder connected to Tomas's?

Card four: Have Hawk do a background check on: Russ Beadle, Tomas's roommate Ty Chambers, Cat's brother Robert Howard, Caitlin Howard, their parents, and the woman in the butterfly dress, Lori Sabal.

Placing the cards near Gar, I phoned Hawk and gave him the list of names. He said he'd have the information ASAP. I assured him I wanted it sooner.

I lifted my cap off Gar's head. "First line of business today—Robert Howard, the dirt bag.

106

15

My aversion to meeting with Robert Howard again was so powerful that I felt like I'd eaten a batch of spoiled raw oysters.

I'd seriously contemplated bringing Gar with me for protection purposes, but at the last minute decided against it. Why put Gar anywhere near such a beast?

All the way to the Howard house, attempting to divert my distaste, I listened to music—Rap—driving, mind-numbing Rap. More than once I had to force the memory of those seven different positions with Jay Mann to the back of my mind.

The same olive-skinned woman let me into the house. Caitlin would not be there of course. Perhaps she would never return, at least when she thought her brother might be home. I took the familiar path to the lanai. Brother Robert met me in a black Spando or was that a Speedo? Whatever. His abs were taut. His broad chest devoid of hair. I wondered if he had it removed. His handshake was flaccid as a scaled fish, his smile a melting cube of ice.

Without being asked, I deposited myself in a seat far from him.

"So what do you want to talk about?" He sunk into a chair near the wrought iron table. His hair was still damp from a swim. A potted palm in a terracotta pot hid half of his face.

"As I said on the phone, your sister."

"Yes, and that made me curious. You barely know my sister."

I had my lie ready. "She's asked me to paint her portrait. And I always find my paintings have more depth if I know more about my subjects." I made a mental note to phone Caitlin and warn her about my white lie.

He frowned, but I was pleased when he shrugged—a sign he accepted my story at least in part.

I withdrew a notebook and a pencil from my breast pocket and held it up. He shrugged again.

"What do you do with your time?"

"What?" His bare feet slipped to the floor. The hand of the wall clock moved.

"Job?"

He gave me a "you're crazy" look. "What does what I do have to do with my sister?"

I smiled at him warmly. "It's just a starting point," I said soothingly.

He lowered his eyelids, but then answered. "I'm an environmental engineering senior."

"Where?"

"Gulf Coast."

"So you see Caitlin often at college?"

"Hardly."

"How would you describe your sister?"

His expression softened. "Intelligent, shy, vulnerable."

I raised my head and smiled at him. "You obviously love her a great deal."

"Of course, she's my sister."

"Not all siblings get along."

"We always have. We're very close."

I let that drop. "What would you say were her favorite things to do?"

"Hmm, besides reading, maybe birds. She loves her birds. She's almost a bird whisperer."

I couldn't help but think of the great blue heron that Gator saw in Tomas's trailer.

"Has she ever had any pet birds?"

He shook his head. "Nah. Folks wouldn't allow it. She just admires them from afar."

Or she has her boyfriend keep one for her.

"Well, thanks, Robert. You've been a great help. I'm sure your sister's portrait will be far more *her* because of you." I replaced my notebook and stood. He rose.

"Oh," I added in an innocent voice, "just out of curiosity, when was the last time you saw Tomas?"

The abrupt switch of directions caught him off guard.

He blanched and stared into my eyes.

"I saw him the night he was found dead. I met him at a bar. He called me and wanted to talk."

I blinked. Ah, telling the truth, how original for a killer. "Was he with anyone?"

Robert flinched.

"Yeah, some guy. But when I arrived, Tomas and I took off."

I gazed steadily at him, eyes smoldering. "And?"

The clock on the walk ticked. He took his own sweet time answering as I planned my quick retreat.

"He was scared."

"Scared?"

"Yeah. He needed some money. Wanted to split the country."

"Did you give him any?" I asked, barely keeping my distain out of my voice.

"Hell, no. The guy was out of his mind. First he stalks my baby sister then he comes to me for money. I mean, what a low-life."

"Blackmail?"

Robert's eyes opened wide. "Blackmail? What are you saying? What would he have on me or my family that could ever cause him to blackmail us?" He took a step back. "Why are you asking all these questions?"

I put up my hands as if to fend off his hostility. "I'm sorry. I've offended you. I guess I was caught up . . . in the . . . uh . . . moment and you got me curious, that's all."

Robert looked at me under lowered eyelids, then went back to his chair and sat. "That dude was a loser. Thank the Lord my sister saw the light and dumped him. Goodbye, Jessie. It's been real."

It wasn't hard to imagine this creep behind bars.

Switching on the car radio, I tapped the steering wheel. "Don't close any suspect doors, woman," I said out loud. "Keep an open mind."

But the fact was, I was positive Robert was the killer.

Caitlin was the key to a sexual predator arrest, but I planned to be the one who proved him a killer. How to do that was still to be known. However, I cautioned myself not to jump to conclusions so early in the investigation. At first, I was sure it was Russ Beadle, now I thought it was Robert Howard. Both speculations were based on emotional dislike, not logical fact. Keeping an open mind was imperative to a successful result, an important lesson of PI 101.

But still . . .

With this in mind, since I had plenty of daylight. I decided that when I returned to Matlacha I'd stop into the kayak rental shop and talk to Lori Sabal—the butterfly dress woman who might have had a thing for Tomas and a motive for murder. Besides, she was expecting me. I needed to get the names of the couple Tomas had taken out on that last kayak tour. Guess I'd take a look at his residence too.

As I drove, I concentrated on country music lyrics, a sort of meditation technique I used to clear my mind of clutter. Clutter tended to thwart my reasoning skills. "Oh, my dog died, my girl left me—woe is me," I warbled. Taking my plastic musical recorder out of the pocket of my door, I toot, toot, tooted all the way back to Matlacha.

Lori was fastening a bungee strap around two kayaks on a rack as I tucked my car into a parking space. She wore cut-offs and a sleeveless, scooped-neck T-shirt. Her auburn hair was pulled behind her ears and hung to her waist. When she saw me she grinned and waved me forward. Beads of water clung to her lower legs and her tennis shoes were soaked.

"Nice day out there, huh?"

"Perfect. Saw more manatee today than all season. The colder weather brought them in."

"Sorry to hear how many we've lost this year," I said.

"Yeah. A pity. Last count was two hundred and ten. Worst red-tide outbreak in years. Blasted government. Every time they open the locks, the phosphates flood the waters. Then the poor manatees' food source is poisoned."

I knew intelligent environmentalists were convinced it was true.

"Guess you're here about Tomas. Come on, we'll look up that information you wanted."

I followed her inside. She went behind a counter. To the left was the restroom near a stack of kayak paddles. She provided the ledger and I flipped open the cover. I found the date of Tomas's death and read: Jim and Cinda Eaton. Half-day tour. Guide: Tomas Moore. Pickup Point: Tarpon Lodge.

Lori yanked open the door of an old fridge. "Water?" She took out two bottles.

I accepted. We went out back and sat at a picnic table not far from an ancient thirteen or fourteen-foot Airstream.

She unscrewed the lid from her bottle, took a long drink and then asked, "How long will you be around?"

I watched a dolphin surface then disappear. "Not that long. My job is waiting for me up north."

"Nice of you to help out the Moores. I know they want some answers. Maybe I can help. Ask away."

"You said you knew nothing about what Tomas was afraid of. Heard anything since the funeral?"

"Nah, afraid not."

"Would it surprise you to know that he went out on a fishing boat as a guide the evening he died?"

111

"Not at all. Tomas was always on the lookout to make more money."

My ears perked up. Another person confirming Tomas's need for money. Shark had said Tomas might be up to something. Surely the story Tomas told Beadle was the truth? Or was it possible Beadle fabricated the tale to protect his young friend? He certainly was capable of that. Russ may not have killed Tomas, but I didn't trust him.

Lori sat her bottle on the table. "Not illegally of course."

"I'd like to find out who the fishermen were. Got any suggestion for me where to start?"

"Hmm. Unfortunately, I haven't heard any rumors, but I'd start with Jimmy at the bait house across from Bert's. He sometimes sets up locals with sport fishermen. If he didn't do it, he'd be able to send you somewhere else."

I thanked her. She asked if I thought the men had anything to do with Tomas's death. I didn't share what I'd learned from Beadle.

"Did Tomas ever talk to you about his girlfriend's brother?"

"Not that I recall."

"No animosity there?"

"Never heard of any."

"You ever meet Tomas's girlfriend?"

Ever so slightly the light in Lori's eyes dimmed. Or was I imagining it?

"Nope. Saw her once in his truck. We waved at each other, but that was it. I got busy with a customer and they left before I was introduced."

I glanced at the trailer. "Where were you the night Tomas died?

"Fort Lauderdale. At my sister's place. It was my niece's birthday."

Interesting how fast she provided her alibi. Fast enough to assume it was solid, as solid as a loving sister's alibi could be trusted.

"Her name is Helen Jarvis if you want to check." She smiled at me. "Not that you're investigating his death or anything."

I finished off my water and set it down. "Is that the trailer Tomas lived in?"

She swiped her hand down the side of her head and nodded.

"Is it locked?"

"Sure. It's still a crime scene, but I've got a key."

"Mind if I take a look?"

"Help yourself, but don't break the tape. I don't need the cops on my butt." The office phone rang again. "I'll be out after I answer that." She stood, drew the key from a pocket and handed it over, then rushed inside. Reluctantly, I went to the trailer.

As I put my flip flop on the metal step, unlocked the door, and slipped under the yellow tape, I remembered the great blue that Gator had seen. It had to have something to do with the bird-loving Caitlin. I opened the door with caution.

The trailer was much as I imagined it would be. Cramped, cluttered, smelling of mildew and burnt popcorn. Ambient light leaking through the slats of the window blinds imposed a shadowy grid on the countertop. Dust hid empty plastic water bottles, a box of cereal, a stack of paper plates, and a stained coffee pot. No powder that Gator had mentioned remained on the stick-legged coffee table. No beer bottles sat on the fold-down table. I went toward an open door and stuck my head into the bathroom and seeing the pattern of dried blood, just as quickly extracted it. In the living room one wall was filled with framed photos. Several showed Tomas with his parents, in two he was with Caitlin, in another he was on the bow of a boat wearing one of those hats like Shark had on to protect his face and neck from the sun. The last one was interesting. Tomas stood beside Lori. Their arms were wrapped around each other. Had they indeed been lovers? Was she a woman scorned? Or was it all conjecture?

As I studied Tomas's image, deep melancholy, heavy as a fisherman's raingear, enveloped me. I touched the photo of Tomas on the boat. Something snapped near the door. Lori's foot on a step. "I'll get to the bottom of this, Tomas. Don't worry," I whispered.

Lori's head popped inside.

"I'm coming out," I said in a rush.

To my relief, she stepped back and I hurried out into the fresh air. "Depressing," I said.

"Yeah, I know. Hard to go in there. I'm selling the trailer. Listen, I called Jimmy. He said to come on over."

Remembering the skeleton, I showed her the picture on my phone. "Reminds me of Mardi Gras," she said.

"Any reason to know why Tomas would give me such a thing?"

"He did?"

"Well, what he did was give it to Gator for safe keeping in case something happened to him."

"Hmm." She studied it. "Can't imagine. Looks sinister though."

I thanked her, asked her to call me if she thought of anything that would help Mariana and walked toward my car. Feet away, I hesitated. "Who has the pet bird?" I asked.

Her eyebrows raised. "Pet bird?"

"The great blue. Gator said there was a great blue in the trailer when he found Tomas."

Lori shook her head. "I don't know anything about a pet great blue. Of course, there's plenty of birds walking around here. You know that."

"That's true." I hesitated, then added: His death is such a shame. Tomas was such a good guy and real attractive, wasn't he?"

Lori blushed. "Yes, he was." Turning, she headed for the office.

"Did you and he…"

She looked over her shoulder and interrupted me. "No. But don't think I didn't try."

I continued to the car deciding I should take Lori off the suspect list. So she was attracted to him and the feeling wasn't mutual? She didn't give off killer vibes. I eased out onto Pine Island Road. An image of Jay in his floor-length white robe came to mind. I felt my cheeks redden and pulled out my cell phone and tapped his number.

"Hi, dinner tonight sounds great. Eight it is."

I pocketed the phone, biting down hard on my lip.

I parked in front of the inn. The bait house was less than a block away. Turning, I went to the edge of the road and paused. A truck whizzed by. I inhaled deeply. Glanced left, then right. Waited until there were no vehicles in my sight, then hightailed it across the pavement. The door to the bait house was open. A clean-shaven, husky man walked out of the back room. We chatted amiably before I asked about Tomas and the trip.

He had not arranged the fishing excursion, but he sent me to another man who he assumed had. I left with his phone number, address, and directions to his place.

The guy lived on Pine Island off Tropical Point. I tapped in his number. He answered on the third ring and immediately told me to call him Big Joe. Knowing that many locals posed for postcards, photos, and paintings, I told him I was a Matlacha artist. I hoped that was enough information to intrigue him. It was. "Sure I'll talk to ya. Come on over. I'll be around the side of the house working on a boat."

Before starting the engine, I phoned Jim and Cinda Eaton, the couple Tomas had taken out kayaking. Tomas, Jim said, was charming and friendly, didn't seem upset in the least. I hated to do it, but I ended by telling him about his murder. I hung up to stunned silence.

When I pulled onto the gravel driveway in front of a one-story shack with a front porch, a five-foot, bowlegged man greeted me. Big Joe? I swallowed my surprise and gave him a cordial smile.

Big Joe's long, frizzy graying hair, bloodshot hazel eyes, and deeply grooved skin stretched tight across his bones made him a sight for any artist seeking a subject matter to behold: Well-worn overalls. A yellowed and stained white T-shirt. Cowboy boots. A rather large, imposing monkey wrench hanging from his right hand. Great. Just great. I kept my eye on it as I climbed out of the car. The hair on the back of my neck itched—had been since seeing Big Joe, a sure sign to be wary. With a hard shove, I slammed the car door. More sound, more power. Worked every time. Sure it did.

Big Joe had a cigarette hanging out of his mouth. He looked me up and down. "Didn't expect no looker," he said with a drawl.

Since I was at least nine inches taller, I leaned back against the car.

He had the muscular physique of a man who had spent most of his life lifting heavy objects. His grip on the wrench was firm. Mid-seventies. Skin weathered by the sun. We shook hands and he suggested we go over there. "Over there" was a narrow strip of ground at the side of the house where a dilapidated wooden boat sat on a rusty trailer and a fire pit was surrounded by logs. Big Joe sat on a log and set the wrench to his right. I took another gnarly seat, facing him. A hot breeze drifted through the mangrove that flanked a narrow lagoon. The smell of rancid, brackish water made me scratch my nose.

"Ever get gators here?" I pulled off my cap and swatted at a swarm of gnats.

"Some." He flicked ashes near his boot.

"Wild pigs?"

"Every night. Got a couple of peacocks that roam around. It's a regular zoo 'round here."

I drew my legs close to my body and kept my eyes on the bank of the lagoon. Then I furrowed my brows at him. "Didn't think there were peacocks running wild here."

He almost hid his grin. "Ain't as dumb as you look."

"You aren't either."

He broke into a broad grin. "Been here nigh onto twenty years. Don't plan to ever move again."

"You a commercial fisherman?"

"Use ta be. Second generation. Since the net ban I do whatever it takes ta make a livin`." He drew in on his cigarette and his cheeks imploded making his head look like a hollowed-out skull. His eyes were large and round, adding to the effect. I thought of Georgia O'Keeffe's skull paintings and realized I had a live specimen facing me who would make a great subject on canvas.

He eyed me up and down. "So, a painter, huh?"

"Yeah."

"Any good?"

I tipped my hand from side to side.

He laughed. "That's `bout the kind of boat repairer I am too. We all can't be no Picasso." He took another drag from his cigarette. "So, how can I help ya?"

I intertwined my fingers. "I'm looking for information about some sport fishermen you may know. They want me to paint a picture for them and I'm not sure I want to take the job."

His eyes narrowed, his expression hardened, and he reached for the wrench. I sat up straighter.

"Who told you that?"

"Jimmy, at the Matlacha fish house, said you might know something, that's all."

"Damn, he's got a flappy tongue."

"Anyway, I was wondering if you could tell me anything that could help me make up my mind."

Big Joe looked toward the lagoon and pulled his earlobe. "I know lots of sport fishermen, damn the luck." He tossed his cigarette butt into the fire pit. "But, those two? A couple of foreign losers. Not too bright."

"Why do you say that?"

"Didn't know a pole from a fish hook."

"So you wouldn't recommend . . . dang their names escape me."

"Alvarez. José and Juan. Brothers."

"Yeah, that's them. So you wouldn't recommend them as paying customers?"

"I took them out once. Those guys were suckers for punishment. They wouldn't give up. We drank a shit load of beer, so it wasn't a total loss. They paid me. No problem." He inspected the monkey wrench.

A rustling sound came from the direction of the lagoon. I blanched and stood. A black cormorant landed on a mangrove branch and spread its wings to dry. No gator slithered forward. When I looked toward Big Joe, he was grinning and puffing away.

"Skittish, ain't ya?"

I smiled sheepishly and sat. My intuition told me to walk softly with any insinuations. Just maybe Big Joe made quite a lot of money on that fishing venture and that was no skin off my Irish back. I fashioned my next question carefully. "Anything exciting happen on that trip?"

He set the wrench across his thighs. "Excitin`?"

Dang. He'd gotten coy on me. I shifted on the log. "Just curious."

"What, little lady, exactly do ya want ta know?"

I looked back toward the lagoon and then at Big Joe. Crossing my legs, I leaned forward. "Someone told me . . ."

"Someone?"

I set both feet on the ground. Big Joe was too fast for me. "*Someone* told me that those guys might be involved with drug running. I don't want to be connected with anyone illegal. But I sure could use the commission, if you know what I mean. Artists like me don't make much money."

Big Joe pulled his pack from the pocket in the front of his overalls and took his time lighting a cigarette before answering. "Drug runnin`, huh?" He gazed into the sky, giving me the impression he was thinking hard or trying to remember something. "Hmm, well, if I recall correctly those fellas were from down South America way. They sure did seem cagey enough." He scratched at his neck and then looked

118

me in the eye. "Now, I ain't sayin' nothin' illegal went on during the time I was with them, mind you. But, the fact is, I wouldn't put nothin' past them two. If I was ya, I'd catch them at the Tarpon Lodge before they take off and tell them to forget it. I'm guessing, they ain't your kind of people."

I studied the undergrowth hoping not to see movement. His words were plenty of confirmation for me to believe Beadle's story. Those sport fishermen were dealing in drugs and using locals to help. Some were innocent, like Tomas. Some were not, like . . .

"Did you happen to give them Tomas's name?"

"Yep."

I attempted to get him to elaborate, but he refused.

I reached for my cell phone.

"I hears you're showin' some dumb skeletal doll picture around. Well, don't show me that. I got enough scary things to deal with without you addin' to it. I don't know nothin' about no hocus pocus. So just don't bother me with it."

I dropped my hand. This was the first time anyone had mentioned this possibility of "hocus pocus." Was it possible there was some religious group practicing on the island that this doll might be connected with? My hunch that these islanders knew more than they were admitting to was panning out. And maybe what it was made them downright edgy, maybe even fearful. I needed somehow to win their trust. But how?

"Hey, do you care if I use you as a subject for a painting?"

Big Joe tossed his head back and laughed. "My ole mug on a canvas? Can't imagine."

"You'd make a great model."

He said he'd think on it.

I left him still sitting on the log. It was dusk. A cloud formation—a robust gator, mouth wide seemed to be slithering across the sky. I hesitated, shut my eyes and saw myself thrashing through the grasses, charging forward— escaping the monster of death that threatened me. Sometimes my imagination was far too vivid and clicked in at the weirdest times.

"Get along, girlie."

I started. It was Big Joe, in shadow beside the shack, holding the wrench.

"Bugs get real thick here about this time a day. They can eat ya alive. Hey, and if you see those two foreigners again, you be real careful, hear me?"

I rushed to my car and was on the road before a gator could blink.

16

Before dressing in anticipation of spending a jittery, uncomfortable night with Jay, I called the Tarpon Lodge and asked if José and Juan Alvarez were still guests. At first, the clerk was reluctant to say they were or weren't. I told her I was a real estate agent in the area who had found the perfect property for them, but I'd misplaced their cell numbers. Since every second person had a realtor's license, she had no problem believing me. She friendly-upped and said they were checking out Saturday. She asked if I wanted to be put through to their room. I said yes, but when she did that, there was no answer. I left my name and number and decided if I went to the lodge early in the morning, I'd most likely catch them. I then made out a note card for Big Joe Smith and Professor Napier. This case was getting a lot more complicated than I expected.

Slipping on my dress, I looked into the mirror. The form fitting fabric showed off my twenty-two-inch waist. Yellow hyacinths complemented my red hair that I'd decided to allow to be free. Even with the sunblock I put on, I couldn't keep my freckles from becoming more prominent in Florida. For this inauspicious occasion, I'd traded my flip flops for heels. I left my room with a heavy step.

I'd never been to this restaurant before, but I'd driven by it many times. It was north of Tom's Town. The outside wasn't much to look at, a painted red building with a large sign, but when we stepped inside I was surprised at how sophisticated the place, the host, and the waitresses were. Black skirts or pants. Black shirts. Sophisticated was not something I'd come across in the area and sophisticated was not something I craved. But this was as good a place as any to end a relationship that should never have begun.

Our appetizer was an asparagus dip with breadsticks and bacon-wrapped scallops. This was followed by Caesar salad, grouper, and brown rice. Our wine—a house Shiraz. I waited for the waitress to leave to tell Jay my news. As we toasted, a man walked toward our table, stopping at my chair.

"Ms. Murphy?" The guy managed to sound like a snake with his pronunciation of "Ms."

A second man in khakis and a flowered shirt sat at a table across the room, watching.

"Yes. And you are?"

He gave his name as José Alvarez.

"The woman at the lodge said you had phoned. I believe she said you were a realtor. Odd. My brother and I are not looking at real estate."

But how did they know I had made the call? Of course, the lodge had my phone number.

Jay looked confused.

Feeling trapped, I leaned back against my chair. "Okay, you're right, you caught me. I fibbed."

Apparently having a flash of inspiration, Jay came to my rescue. He patted my fingers. "Now, honey, were you doing it again? Shame on you." He shook his head in mock disapproval. "Sir, this beautiful lady is a Matlacha hooker."

The man's eyebrows shot up. Not hiding his amusement, he looked from Jay to me.

I was staring in disbelief at Jay.

Jay continued. "Now don't get the wrong idea. She's not a prostitute. The hookers are a community service group. Their contributions help many on the islands. Be careful, my

122

man, she's soliciting money again." He turned to me and spoke as if to a naughty child. "Jessie, really!"

Alvarez almost smiled, but not quite. I could have kissed Jay for his quick thinking. I made my expression appear sheepish, even covering my eyes as if I was embarrassed. "Oh, I'm so sorry. I should never have lied. But, you know how it is, no one likes a person asking for money. The clerk would never have given me your phone number if I told her I was seeking contributions. Oh, how embarrassing."

The guy motioned to the other man to join us then sat. "So, little lady, what's your cause?"

Luckily for me, the other guy's arrival and introduction gave me time to think. I came up with the idea of a scholarship fund for local kids in Tomas's honor. But before I could open my mouth, the second man leaned across the table, lowered his voice and said, "We know you're investigating Tomas Moore's death." Both men, glanced right to left, then showed us FBI badges.

"We also know that you know we went fishing with Moore the night he died."

I was speechless.

The FBI were the sport fishermen?

The man continued. "When the kid left the boat so quick, we knew he was scared and not a regular. The captain of the delivery boat knew him. I heard them talkin`. We planned to interrogate him the following day, but he didn't make it that long."

The second agent took over. "We're working on finding out who the captain was. The boat, of course, was camouflaged. Name on registration was fake. We'll get him, don't you worry. And when we do, we'll have that kid's killer as well." He put his hands on the table and pushed himself up. "We're asking you to stop nosing around. You're complicating our case." The second man stood. "Good evening, kids. Enjoy the rest of your night."

They walked away.

123

"Well, now," Jay said, "That was exciting. Right out of the movies. Your life is definitely more interesting than mine."

I raised my eyebrows at him and assured him that this didn't happen to me often.

"So, will you quit the investigation?"

I shrugged. "Who am I? The FBI think they know who the killer is, right?"

"So they say."

We ate a few seconds in silence and then I broached the subject I wanted to raise with Jay.

"What happened the other night . . ." I hesitated.

"Yes."

"It can't happen again."

Jay looked crestfallen. "Can't? Or you won't let it?"

"You know as well as I that I'm leaving soon. It's ridiculous to start a relationship now."

"Have you heard of phones and airplanes?"

I set down my wine. "I *don't* want this to continue," I said. "It's over."

His lips drew into a firm line. Ducking his head, he muttered something under his breath and picked up his fork.

17

I figured I'd leave finding the captain of the drug-running boat up to the FBI. These guys were way out of my league. The captain was most likely the killer. My investigation was over. It was time to report to the Moores. They deserved knowing what I'd found out about their son's last couple of days. I'd take my power walk, shower, phone them, and hopefully see them this morning or at the very least sometime today.

Luck was with me. Both Moores would be home all day. I set up a one p.m. meeting. That would give me time for lunch and maybe a little sketching. Anymore, I hated to let too many hours pass without some creative release. I was twenty-eight and figured I'd lost enough time not taking my art seriously. My goal was to get my work to the public. My carrot wasn't money. It was to share parts of myself with others. One brief word of praise was all I needed as motivation. In fact, I didn't even need that anymore. If I didn't draw or paint, I started to get down.

Ending the budding relationship with Jay was the right thing to do. Period. I had been weak. It would not be repeated.

After my exercise, I showered, made a plate of fruit, summer sausage, cheese and crackers and settled on an Adirondack chair facing the soothing sea. Placing my flip flops on the railing I leaned my sketchpad against my bent legs. I didn't have anything particular in mind to draw. I just placed my charcoal pencil on the paper and made the first stroke, then let my sight and hand do the rest. I loved the freedom involved in the process. Slowly, I sunk inward. The sea receded. The continuous snarl of rubber tires over the serrated metal of the drawbridge muffled to a whimper. I didn't look up. Not sideways. Not anyways. No ways. Gently, I rubbed the texture of the paper.

"Hey, Jessie Murphy."

The three words were pronounced bluntly and were surrounded in a furious climate of anger, making me cringe. Hand arrested in mid-stroke, I looked in the direction of the speaker.

"What do you want, Beadle?"

He charged forward. "Who gave you the right to use my name?"

"Excuse me!"

"You've been telling people that I told you that Tomas was trafficking in drugs."

I pushed out of the low chair. "I did no such thing."

"You fool. This is a small community. Word gets around fast. Nobody wants to blacken Tomas's name."

"That's ridiculous."

He stomped forward, stopping way too close for comfort. The chair was behind me. I couldn't back up. "I'll tell you what, girlie. You won't get another word out of me and doubtful from anyone else." He glowered at me, turned on his heels, and was gone faster than he had come.

Good thing I didn't need more information. Good thing the feds had everything under control. Good thing.

But I was stunned. All I could imagine was that those agents had started the rumor. Dammit. Why? To get me fired? I wasn't planning to proceed. If the Moores heard this, they'd probably refuse to pay me for all the hours and gas I'd put into the investigation. Pissed, I went inside and dialed the lodge. I wanted to give those suckers a solid piece of my Irish anger. The men had checked out. Figured. Thanks, jerks.

Still fuming, I hitched up my courage, phoned the Moores and told them I was running late. I was reassured when Marianna's voice was as warm as ever.

It was twelve forty-five. As an afterthought, I contacted Zen to see if she could join me. Fortunately, she could. I wanted to give them my report before they heard the rumor I supposedly spread about Tomas and I wanted Zen there to back me up.

On the way, I told Zen about Beadle's outburst. She said I was lucky he hadn't tossed me in the pass.

18

Mariana and Shorty sat on the front porch. A red paisley scarf covered most of Mariana's black hair. Shorty wore jeans and an orange T-shirt. They were holding hands, but as we climbed out of the car, they released their fingers and slid apart.

I put my foot on the first rickety step and gulped at Shorty's expression. It was wooden. A rifle lay across his lap. Mariana had been crying. Eww. I hesitated. Zen did the same.

There was a brief silence, the kind that I imagined occurred between the trigger being pulled on a shotgun and the blast.

"So shoot her," Zen said. "Go on. Get it over with."

At which point Shorty's facial muscles relaxed. He didn't smile or anything, but he did motion for us to sit in the porch swing. I completed the climb with my eyes on the steps.

No one but Zen would have come up with that comment. But Zen was so good-spirited and so without guile she could get away with almost anything. Zen had a heart of gold and would do anything for anyone she liked. A couple of nights ago she'd shared her story. She'd been raised on the streets of Chicago and at fifteen barely missed a bullet from the owner of a pawn shop her gang robbed. She'd spent two years in juvenile detention and emerged a believer in everything New

Age. While in prison, she received her first tat—a Celtic knot positioned at the base of her spine.

Her parents brought her to Matlacha weeks after her release. Although they'd died in a car accident a year later, she'd stayed—first with foster parents on Pine Island, ending up in Matlacha when she turned eighteen. "The island," she'd said, "is my soulmate."

How a land mass could be a soulmate, Zen couldn't explain, but she said there were lots of things that couldn't be explained. Everyone knew that. Along with this, Zen was fearless, which was a handy quality to have, what with the presence of the rifle and the charged emotions.

Shorty waited until we sat before he said, "Our son *never* dealt in drugs."

Mariana burst into tears. Zen gave the swing a slight push.

I leaned forward, clasping my hands between my knees. "Before I came here today, I heard that someone started the rumor that I said that. I hoped to get to you before you heard it. But Shorty, Mariana, why would I say such a thing? You hired me to find your son's killer. Why would I defame his name?"

Shorty threw his arm over his sobbing wife's shoulder and pulled her close, gazing at me steadily.

His glance shot from me to Zen. "Talk," he said. "And it better be good."

I told him Beadle's story—that Tomas had possibly and unwittingly been part of a transfer of drugs from one boat to another and that upon getting to shore scared, had run without payment.

Mariana's sobs became louder.

"You think someone involved killed our son to keep him quiet?"

Unfortunately, I couldn't tell him about the FBI connection or reveal their speculation.

"I can't give you the details yet, but it's highly possible." Why had those feds spread that rumor? Something wasn't right. I came thinking I would tell the Moores that my investigation was over, but my neck hairs itched every time I pictured those federal dudes' faces. I tapped my foot. It was definitely not time to leave everything up to those guys, feds or not. I had leads to follow. Motives to explore. A killer to find.

Shorty studied the plank floor.

"Listen," I said, "I promise you that I'll do the best I can to give out no information about the case but to you two—that wouldn't be professional and certainly wouldn't help my investigation. Since these are small islands and I am talking to several people, rumors fly. But I'm human and not a professional PI. Mistakes can be made. Please phone anytime you have a concern. I'm on your side."

Shorty said nothing.

I continued, talking fast. "I've told no one that I'm investigating this case. Besides you, only Zen, Gator, and Jay Mann know for sure what I'm doing." But they were sworn to secrecy. Again, I couldn't mention the FBI. Many suspected of course. Like Shark and Lori Sabal, but that was to be expected. "As far as anyone else goes, I'm a family friend getting information to help you get through the grieving process." I leaned closer. "There's some confusion about Tomas and Cat. I'm not sure who broke up with whom or if they actually ever broke up. Do you know anyone who was close enough to them who might know the real story?"

Mariana bit her lip, then shook her head.

Shorty's eyebrows furrowed. "Why does it matter if they were still seeing each other or who broke up with who?"

"It may not. Or, it may."

"If Tomas broke up with that gal, you think she might have killed him?"

"I'm not eliminating any possibilities."

"Hey!" Shorty's face transformed into an angry mask.

Mariana straightened in her chair. "Now, Shorty, calm down. That girl couldn't kill a bug. Don't you go start thinkin' otherwise." She looked at me. "I don't know their friends, but I would ask his roommate or other college friends."

"I've already talked to his roommate and heard his story. Your son doesn't seem to have had any other college friends. You ever meet the roommate?"

"No, never. Tomas, in fact, as I recall, never talked about him." Mariana's eyes were downcast.

Shorty's face had paled. He interrupted me. "Me neither. Didn't I read that someone at that university was just shot?"

Why had they both just lied about Ty Chambers? They had, I was sure. Maybe they just didn't like to connect him with their son.

"Yeah. In fact, I was on campus when it happened. It was Tomas's adviser. I'd just talked to her."

"You think there's a connection?" Mariana asked.

"I don't know. Again, it's possible."

"Maybe she was involved in the drug running. Maybe she knew who killed Tomas and was killed before she could rat them out," Shorty said.

"Sounds crazy, but it's a possibility."

We were silent for several seconds. I decided not to mention my theory about Robert Howard, but I did have another question. "Did Tomas ever talk to you about Cat's brother, Robert?"

Shorty shrugged and shook his head.

Mariana paled.

"What did he say?"

Shorty looked perplexed as he looked at his wife. Mariana glanced furtively at him before beginning to speak. "Tomas was not one to talk negative about people. I always told him if you don't have anything good to say about someone, then don't say anything. But he had nothin' good to say about Cat's brother. I overheard him talkin' on the phone to Cat, oh, I don't know how long ago, and he mentioned the cops. Then he lowered his voice so much I couldn't hear him. After he hung up I asked him what that was all about. He said that it was a matter between him and Cat. It was confusin' 'cause I was sure he said something like: We need to turn him in to the cops."

"You never told me that," Shorty said.

Mariana hung her head.

What she said convinced me that Cat hadn't lied. She had told Tomas about the abuse—and it was possible he had threatened Robert with arrest, a strong motive for murder.

I asked them to keep what I told them to themselves. They agreed and Zen and I left. As I slid behind the wheel, I saw Shorty and Mariana were holding hands again. Mariana's head rested on Shorty's broad shoulder.

Slamming my door, I started the engine and switched on the car's air. "Thanks a lot," I said to Zen.

"For what?"

"Telling Shorty to shoot me."

Zen chuckled. "Anytime, sweetie, anytime."

It grated on me that Zen had just used the nickname Grandma Murphy had dubbed me. Sweetie. It especially bothered me because Zen was so smug and lighthearted with her reply. Always so sunny.

I shifted into reverse, grinding the gears. "Shorty might have done it," I mumbled.

"Might of. Could of. Would of. Didn't," she said. "So, who's your prime suspect?"

"I'm not sure." Robert Howard's face materialized but I wasn't in the mood to discuss specifics with Zen. I switched on the radio and we listened to music until I slowed and parked in front of her door.

"I have a bad feeling about Russ Beadle," Zen said.

"According to Beadle, everyone has a bad feeling about him."

"It's not just the bad boy thing."

"Okay. What?"

"I'm thinking you better find Tomas's killer before he does. He doesn't have any respect for the law. Keep your eyes on your back. If Beadle thinks you found the killer, he just might walk over you to get to him first."

I let out a puff of air. "Okay, I'm warned."

Zen opened the car door. "Don't let the bed bugs bite, especially under that billowing white robe."

"Hey!"

"Didn't think I knew, did ya?" She whooped and ran.

I watched her go, kicking myself that I had forgotten to mention the skeleton doll to the Moores. Damn. I'd have to take care of that soon. Mariana surely knew something about such a symbol and what it might mean to her son.

Shaking my head, I reversed, hit a rut and cringed with the resulting bone-jarring bounce.

19

Chablis in hand, I phoned Hawk. Perhaps, just perhaps, people on campus were involved in drug dealing. Hawk answered on the first ring. I learned:

1. Ty Chambers had been arrested on marijuana possession last year, but with the help of an expensive lawyer, charges were dropped. Age 21.

2. Sarah Peters was born in Colombia. She'd come to the states to get a Ph.D. where she met her husband and became naturalized. Mother and sister lived somewhere in Florida. Age 37.

3. Lori Sabal had no record. Was born in New Jersey. Married three times. Age 52.

4. Tobin Peterson had been a Lee County deputy for ten years. Age 39.

5. David Napier was unmarried. Tenured. Been at Gulf Coast U since it opened. Age 58.

6. Robert Howard. No record. Age 24.

7. Caitlin Howard was a former valedictorian. Spent a year up north. Hawk was still checking on that. No record. Age 20.

8. Russ Beadle had been imprisoned five times. First three on misdemeanors. The fourth time in the 80s drug bust

in the Everglades. Fifth time for assault with a deadly weapon—cracked the skull of a man with a bottle in a bar fight. Age 65. Commercial fisherman and crabber.

Before hanging up, I asked Hawk to check on the supposed FBI agents and Big Joe Smith. Hawk assured me that the FBI agent check would be tricky, since it sounded like they were working undercover. The names had to be false. I asked if he could find out at least if there was an active drug investigation going on in the islands. He said he'd do what he could, but not to be hopeful.

"Keep your nose clean, Jess. We expect you up here by Jacob's birthday."

"I'll be there, don't worry. This case isn't going to take another month." I pocketed my phone.

But I still had no answers. No proof of anything. No concrete motive. Only weak speculation. Mostly I ran into doors, not windows. I wondered where my thinking had veered left.

I heard a noise coming from the dock. I took another sip of wine. Sounded like someone had arrived by boat. Odd. I went to the window and peered out.

It was a cloudy night. No moon. Few visible stars. The far islands were draped in shadow. "Who's there?"

BAM!

The lamp near my shoulder exploded.

20

"Now, Zen," I said, "don't go all emo on me. We don't know anyone shot at me deliberately. In fact, we're not even sure it was a shot."

"I have every right to go emo. How can you be so calm?"

"We don't," I repeated stubbornly, "know it was a bullet."

It was of course.

Zen powered out of the chair I'd insisted she'd sit in. "Say it *was* a bullet. Say someone is trying to kill you. What will you do?"

We were waiting for the cops—touching nothing—not disturbing the evidence. Once they arrived, we'd know soon enough.

"Well, the good thing is . . ."

"GOOD thing, you're kidding, right?" Zen, the always look-on-the-bright-side-woman, was staring at me as if I'd grown two more heads. Funny how we'd switched roles. Now I was being the optimist.

"I'm still alive."

I wanted everyone—Zen, the cops, Jay when he arrived—to think I was calm as a cradled baby, that having a shot whiz past me and shatter the lamp hadn't fazed me. I didn't want the cops assigning me a bodyguard or watching my every move. I'd managed to call Zen and my voice had broken, and she got here in less than ten minutes.

"Someone was most likely shooting at something in the water from their boat and got careless, that's all."

"Oh, yeah?" Zen began to pace. "I find out you're right and when I find them, I'll cram their gun down their throat 'til they gag."

Sirens and flashing lights screamed cop arrival.

Zen was asked to wait on the dock while they took my report. She didn't hear me inform them about the boat. Nor could she hear me tell them that the departing boat's engine was loud, even from beneath the table I had dived under. They were not happy about my insistence that I didn't need protection.

They left with a warning to keep the window and door closed.

Zen hurried in, then eyed me. "Well?"

I crossed the room. "I'm starved. Times like this I turn gluttonous." I yanked open a cabinet and pulled out an unopened package of Oreos. "Want one?" I asked, tearing at the plastic.

Zen took the carton of milk out of the fridge. "I like mine dunked. You?"

"Oh, yeah."

"Bullet?"

"Uh, huh."

We ate like the cookie monster was standing over our shoulders.

"I think," I began, wiping crumbs from my lips, "there's that other factor to consider."

Zen's dripping cookie wavered over the milk.

"Tomas's adviser on campus. I talk to her. She's murdered. Maybe there's a connection."

"Drugs?" Zen popped the whole cookie into her mouth.

"I wonder if Ty Chambers owns a boat."

"Tomas's roommate?"

I nodded, musing.

"So, what's next?" Zen's white mustache made me smile. "I got laid off tonight. Just think of me as your shadow. You go somewhere. I go. Me . . . Click. You . . . Clack."

I finished off another cookie. If the shooter thought he was going to scare me off, he knew nothing about the Murphy clan.

The first person I wanted to talk to again was Ty Chambers.

"Ever been to Gulf Coast University?" I asked.

21

Before leaving for the university I wrote down my thoughts on the case—one fact and speculation per card:

- Tomas discovered dead in bathroom by Gator night he returns from fishing trip frightened. Feared retribution? Most likely. But fishermen were feds, so possibly the captain is the murderer. But I don't think so.
- Tomas left me—an almost stranger—an envelope with a skeleton doll dressed up like a woman. Perhaps his warning to me that I could be in serious danger if I took his case?
- Great blue in trailer/door unlocked. Caitlin loves birds.
- Cocaine on coffee table with two half-filled bottles of beer.

I tapped the card. I was missing a detail here. What was it? I glanced at Zen. She didn't raise her head. Her T-shirt was brown and embossed with a fish. Ah, hah, the beers were a specialty—ah, Dogfish Head Ale—that's right. The same beer I'd seen Caitlin drinking the night before the funeral. I jotted this down. Then:

- Tomas goes to Beadle afraid, then to mom. Never meets up with dad.
- Tomas—goal-oriented student who recently broke up with Caitlin. If Tomas had disappointed her, was she

139

crazy enough or enraged enough to kill him? Doubtful.
But possible.

- Tomas needed more money to pay for college. Worked
for crabber, Russ Beadle, keeping it secret from his
parents. Why? Works two other jobs. Why?
- Dad is a crabber. Mom a Mexican who has a thing for
owls.
- Tomas, an A-driven student, missed two pop quizzes in
class he took about the role of crabbers and fisher folk in
drug bust of late 80s. Why?
- Adviser who seemed real nervous talking about Tomas
murdered less than two hours after I spoke to her.
Colombian ancestry. Wore owl-decorated jewelry.
- Tomas's roommate describes beautiful girlfriend as
mousy. Why? Projects different to different people?
- Girlfriend claims bro is abusing her and she told Tomas.
True? Probably what upset Tomas. Tomas and bro have
confrontation night of death. Motive: Jealous rage.
- Killer: Robert Howard.

Now, how to prove it? But first, be smart, confirm Cat's
story. I hear you Grandma, don't worry.

22

"Well, now, I'm not sure how I should answer that."

We were sitting in Napier's office, hoping to convince him to talk about another student. Anyway, *I* was working hard while Zen inspected her fingernails.

Napier spoke with measured words. "It's not that Caitlin is a registered student. With permission, she audits courses." Napier tipped his head, looking at the stack of disheveled papers on his desk. "I think," he said slowly, "I *can* confidently give you some answers without compromising my position." His gaze shot to me and then to Zen. "As long as this conversation is confidential, of course."

I assured him that was the case.

Napier was not too fond of the Howards. Not, that is, after how they'd treated their son once he came out of the closet. I hoped I took the news that Robert was gay without a hint of surprise. I was glad my eyes had been directed at the floor as my startled look would have given me away. A gay brother sexually assaulting his sister? I don't think so. Caitlin's story was being shot full of holes the size cannon balls would make.

All I had to do was occasionally grunt or nod my head and Napier was willing to charge onward.

If the young man survived the shame his parents put him through unscathed, Napier said, he'd be surprised.

"So you had Robert Howard as a student too?"

"I did. In fact, he came to me and asked for advice about coming out. It is a known fact on campus that I am gay. My partner teaches in the philosophy department. Robert was worried he'd be disinherited. Fortunately that didn't happen, but his parents took it hard. They wanted him to see a psychiatrist. In fact, they tried to kidnap him to force his admittance into an institution, but luckily, Robert fought them off successfully. It's sad. Parents panic sometimes. It's amazing how many people still believe that being gay is a mental disease." Napier shook his head in disgust. "He stayed with us for a month or two while his parents calmed down and began to get the counseling they needed to accept who their son was."

"And his sister? You said she had few friends? You felt sorry for her."

"Yes, that's right. She's a special case."

"In what way?"

"She's brilliant for one. But, she has a, well, a bit of a problem."

Sensing Zen was going to speak up, I sent her a warning glance. Luckily, she got my message and resumed her nail inspection.

Napier reached toward a stack of papers and began straightening them. "I'm so disorganized," he mumbled. Setting the now neat stack in front of him, he added, "She lives in a bit of a, ah, fantasy world." He bit down on his lower lip. "I really don't think I should say anything else. She may be readmitted to the university next semester. It wouldn't be right."

"Oh, but of course, she was *only* auditing your class."

A flash of uneasiness came and went in his eyes before he said, "Why, yes, true. However, the charges against her may be dropped."

That last sentence apparently was a slip Napier wished he hadn't made. He refused to say anything more. I pulled my phone out of my pocket and showed him the skeleton doll.

"Ah, you should google those. Their use is quite fascinating," he said.

"I already have, but what I was wondering was if Tomas or any other student had talked to you about them."

He looked startled. "Why, yes. In fact, Tomas brought almost this very photo to me. I said the same thing to him I said to you. I'm afraid my focus is very narrow right now. My research, you know."

Minutes later, Zen and I left the office and then the building keeping step with one another.

"Sounds like Tomas might have stumbled onto something that concerned him," Zen said.

"Yeah, it does. I'm starting to think there's religious activity surrounding this symbol on the islands." Maybe, I thought, this is what made so many locals fidgety. But Zen denied having any knowledge of it. Odd.

"I'd like to meet this girlfriend of Tomas's. She sounds like a real gem. Maybe she's part of this secret group."

"I'd forgotten you hadn't met her."

"From all I'm hearing, it's hard to believe a level-headed kid like Tomas would have anything to do with her. Charges? Hot dang."

Caitlin's innocent eyes and rounded shoulders came to mind. "She has a way of getting under your skin," I said. By now, I was pretty disgusted with myself. At first I'd believed everything Caitlin had said. No wonder she wouldn't go to the cops with me to accuse her brother of sexual abuse. I wondered what Robert had done to make his sister accuse him. In Bert's, he had seemed her protector. What kind of person would falsely accuse a brother of sexual abuse? I hated to think. I hesitated. "How do you find out why someone was booted from a university?" I took off my cap and rubbed my forehead with the back of my hand. "The dean of students would know, but I'm sure there's some code of silence that would have to be enforced." I nestled my cap on my tousled locks again. "Do you suppose they have a campus newspaper?"

We headed for the posted map and found the listing: Gulf Coast Press, Lutgert Hall, Room 352.

An Asian young man, a coed with blonde cropped hair, and a stocky, sandy-haired student looked up as Zen and I burst into the room through double swinging doors. The newsroom was partitioned off into cubicles containing computers and monitors on three-foot desks. Framed feature articles, journalist awards, and photos of past and current student journalists lined one wall. An American flag hung from a pole on a stand. Someone was eating fries. The smell made my stomach gurgle. Gentle chords of New Age music filled the room creating an unexpected sense of peacefulness. I caught the eye of the female and went toward her, Zen following. The stocky guy resumed typing on his keyboard. The Asian reached into a bag and extracted a three-inch fry while staring at his screen.

My questions to the coed about scandals were met with a suggestion that we go to the library where all past newspaper issues were archived and could be found on any of the public computers in a lab on the second floor. The entire staff were freshmen. She hadn't heard or read anything about any recent situation that had caused the dismissal of students. Last year's news was old news as far as she was concerned. Raising her voice, she asked the question of her peers. They shook their heads. I thanked her.

At the library, it took me less than half an hour to find what I was looking for. "Whoa, listen to this."

Zen turned away from the game of computer solitaire she'd been playing.

"Student Paper Scandal Rocks Campus. Three students dismissed after accused of being involved in campus-wide cheating scam. Last fall an anonymous tip alerted authorities that three students were writing and selling student papers. An extensive undercover investigation revealed the organized ring were charging $200 per paper. Students involved were dismissed. Those who bought the papers are warned that such behavior will not be tolerated. Other dismissals may be in the offing. No names will be revealed. Acts of plagiarism will be treated under a "no tolerance" policy."

"Ah, hah!" Zen said. "Looks like we know how our brilliant, rich bitch who can't even bother to come to her boyfriend's funeral, spends her spare time."

"Hey, her grandpa had been rushed to the hospital."

"Oh, yeah, I've heard that one before," Zen said, rolling her eyes.

Unfortunately, I was afraid Zen was right. I'd been hoodwinked big time.

Still . . .

"Anyway, the girl's from a family with money. Why would she get involved in such a scheme?"

"Maybe her folks are stingy."

I turned back to the computer. "Maybe there's another scandal we haven't found yet," I mumbled.

But an hour later I tapped "End Session" and leaned back in my chair. Zen did the same.

"So far, it's the only possibility."

It looked like possibly, just possibly, Caitlin Howard was a pathological liar *and* a cheat. And I was a first-class fool.

"You suppose when Tomas found out she was involved in the scheme and was thrown out of this ole university, he dropped her like a hot tator?"

I stared at Zen, considering. Could be. Tomas sure wasn't the type to condone cheating.

"Cause if he did, I bet that would make her real mad."

Wasn't Caitlin a bird lover? Wasn't there a great blue heron in Tomas's trailer? Click. Click.

I jumped out of the chair. "Come on. We've got work to do."

Click.

23

When we walked out of the library, the day had turned gray and gloomy, which made it harder to kick my bad mood. I hated to have heavy wool pulled over my eyes and lately it seemed it was happening all too often. My head was throbbing. I gave some thought to calling Hawk to ask if he'd learned why Caitlin had spent time up north. But if he'd learned anything, he would have called.

Zen was staying so close to my side that I began to feel suffocated. I stepped away. Robert Howard was no longer my Number One suspect. In fact, I felt bad for him. No one deserved to be falsely accused. Then I told myself to stop feeling bad about anyone. Who the killer was, was still up for grabs. I needed to stop jumping too quickly to emotion-based conclusions.

In the car Zen said, "I've been thinkin`."

Oh, no.

I switched on the engine. "Yeah?"

"You think we should carry guns?"

I cringed. "No!" I said, backing out. "We do that we're asking for trouble. You got a license to carry?"

She shook her head.

"Didn't think so."

"Seems to me, we're surrounded by trouble," she mumbled. "Did you hear about the other excitement on Pine Island last night?"

I glanced her way, then passed a truck loaded with palm trees.

"Big Joe was robbed."

My ears perked up.

"Oh man, he was pissed. You should have heard him at Bert's last night. I can't imagine why anyone broke into his house. That ole goat don't own nothin` worth stealin`."

I gave Zen all the attention a driver could. Someone robbed Big Joe on the same night I was shot at? I slammed on the brakes, then passed a Chevy.

Zen rolled down her window. "Sure hope the sun pops back out. I hate gray skies."

"Big Joe have any idea who robbed him?"

"Nah."

"Cops get any fingerprints?"

Zen laughed. "Cops? You're jokin`, right? Big Joe wouldn't invite no cops onto his property."

Duh. Some surprise.

I parked in front of my place. "Thanks for coming along," I told Zen. "You don't need to come in."

Zen looked right then left. "The hell I don't," she said. I'll be sleepin` here tonight."

Zen opted for the first shower. "Lock the doors. I'll be done before you open two beers."

I took my cap off, smoothed my hair, and put it back in place. I wanted to talk to Big Joe. And not with Zen's ears in attendance. I waited until I could hear the beat of the shower, snatched up the car keys and the camera I used for important stuff and then hurried out the door.

24

Big Joe was sitting on his porch, rifle draped across his knees. His head leaned to the left. Snoozing? I slid the strap of my camera over my head and shut my car door with care. No sense startling a sleeping man holding a rifle.

When I put my flip flop on the bottom step of his porch, Big Joe's eyes shot open and he looked around before concentrating on me: "What ya want?" he snarled.

Seems getting robbed hadn't made Big Joe any more hospitable. This guy needed a woman. I wondered what he'd think of my grandma. My Grandma Murphy with this curmudgeon? The poor guy wouldn't know what hit him.

I sat on the top step. I wanted to talk to Big Joe again, then Mariana Moore.

"Hoped you wouldn't mind if I took some pictures. The painting, remember?"

"I ain't much in the mood," he said.

I continue to look at him.

"Ah, go ahead. Guess I ain't much in a good mood most of the time."

I thanked him and began snapping photos. He truly would be an excellent model for a painting, maybe even more than one.

"You ever been married?" I asked.

"Forty years. She died a couple of years back."

"Ah, I'm sorry."

He lit a cigarette and showed me his profile. I snapped and snapped.

"You must have been thrilled when Tomas Moore fell in love."

Big Joe sighed and inhaled deeply. "You bet. The boy deserved the best."

"Yeah, Caitlin Howard is a real nice gal."

"Like I said, the best."

"Did you talk to her often?" I stood and walked to the end of the porch, continuing to capture different angles.

"Often enough," he said. "He brought her out here off and on." He nodded to a picnic table under a shade tree. "They used ta sit under that tree and study some. You can bet they moon-eyed each other most of the time."

"I've heard she's real smart."

"Oh, yeah. Tomas was proud of that. Used ta say she was the smartest gal on campus."

"I heard she started college a year late. She talk to you about that?"

Big Joe tapped his cigarette and ashes fell onto his rifle butt. He whisked them off. "That girl had troubles. Any fool could see that. Her folks had her committed 'cause she fell for the gardener."

"You're kidding?"

"That gal's no more nuttier than I am. You know how rich folks are? If you don't do what they want, they use their money to get it. Rich folks. They got their strange ways." He tossed his cigarette butt off the porch.

"But she was able to start college the following year?"

"The gardener was an illegal. He was sent back to Colombia. Got hisself killed a few months later."

"Wow, that's a sad story."

"Life's a bitch," he said, "and then ya die."

"Do you still see her?"

"Not since the night the kid di…was murdered."

"She was here then?"

"Sitting right at that table helping me clean fish."

I looked at the wooden table imagining Big Joe and Caitlin talking while they worked.

"Hell, if Tomas hadn't called her, we'd of eaten together. But ya know young love. She talked ta him and was up and gone like a dove for a worm."

"So she went to his place?"

He shrugged, then made that odd chuckling noise again. "She had a hell of a time getting that great blue in the back of the truck."

My red flags caught the wind. "Great blue?"

"Ya didn't know about that? She was tight with it as she was with Tomas. I never saw her without Einstein. You should of seen them when they were walkin`. They both looked like they owned anything they touched."

"I guess Tomas kept the bird since she was in college?" I kept my tone casual.

He looked disgusted. "How could he do that? He was in college too?"

"So you kept it? Can I see it?" I raised my camera.

"Girl, you ain't thinkin` right. Do I look like a bird sitter?"

Feeling sheepish, I focused the camera, clicking shots of his yard.

"You know anything about any secret religious practice going on around here?"

I could tell that question took him off guard. He sniffed and changed the subject. "You ever captain a boat?"

"Couple of times," I said.

He chuckled, but his chuckle was more a rickety grumbly sound than most you hear. "You gals today. You do it all. I woulda bet ten bucks that Cat couldn't steer a go-cart and what does she do—we take her out and she takes over. She's a natural on water. Turned out she'd been captaining a boat since she was ten. Never woulda guessed. Hell, you ladeez are a surprise every minute. My wife couldn't even clean a fish, let alone run no boat. Ya know how to clean a fish?"

I shook my head.

150

He set down his rifle and stood. "Reckon I've had enough pictures took."

It hadn't passed my notice that Big Joe never returned to my question about any secret religious goings on.

25

The Moores' kitchen was small with red cabinets, white porcelain knobs, squares of pebble-patterned vinyl on the floor. A wooden table big enough for four sat in front of a checkered-red curtain-covered window. Mariana had dark circles under her eyes. She was dressed in black and wore a beaded necklace with a pendant in the shape of an owl. Her hand shook as she placed a coffee mug in front of me. The mug was decorated with a bright brown, orange, and black barn owl.

I patted her hand. "How are you doing?"

She gazed out the window. "As good as can be expected. You're not supposed to survive your kids." She caught my eye. "Have you proved my boy wasn't takin` drugs yet?"

I thought it was odd that her question was directed at the drug accusation rather than toward whether I was any closer to finding the killer, but I supposed it was a matter of family pride and respect for her son's memory.

"Nothing yet. I'm sorry. When will Shorty be home?"

She shot a look to the wall clock. "Not for another half-hour."

I took a sip of coffee. "You really care about Tomas's girlfriend, don't you?"

The dull light in Mariana's eyes darkened even more. "I thought they were perfect together. I can't believe she hasn't come to see me."

"She hasn't?"

Mariana let out a small sound, one that a hurt kitten might whimper. I reminded myself to be gentle.

"I'm trying to get a better sense of Caitlin. Do you mind telling me about their relationship?"

"Not at all. She and Tomas met just before a weekend he was to come home for his uncle's birthday party. He couldn't stop talking about her. He was really impressed with her intelligence and the fact she wasn't a makeup queen. He said she didn't need makeup to be a beauty. The men made fun of him for being so obviously starry-eyed so fast, of course. But he didn't care."

"When did you meet her?"

"About two weeks later. He brought her home on a Saturday. We had a crab bake. She was so nice. She pitched right in. I liked her from the start. But not Shorty. He said something was odd about her."

"And you had no idea they broke up?"

"None. Sometimes folks are the last to hear."

Mariana began wringing her hands and I was beginning to feel guilty about all my questions. She reached behind her and pulled a tissue out of a box on the counter that sat in front of several used white candles. "Sorry," she said, dabbing her eyes, then blowing her nose.

"Did Tomas or Caitlin ever tell you anything about her year after she graduated from high school?"

"Oh, what a dreadful thing to happen to someone. My heart went out to the girl. What a horrible thing for parents to do to a child." She went on to relate the same story Big Joe told me about the gardener.

I pulled my cell phone from my pocket and showed her the skeleton photo. She blanched and looked away.

"Tomas left me this," I said. "The sheriff has it now. Do you know what the significance is?"

153

She lowered her head and shook it from side to side.

She knew something. That was obvious.

"Are you sure you don't know anything? Because, Mariana, you sure look and act like you do."

Her moist eyes sought mine. "When Tomas was a kid we gave him one of these for his birthday. He always cherished it. It's upsetting to know he gave it away."

"You have no idea why he would leave it for me?"

"None at all."

A plausible story? Well, kind of . . . sort of . . . I changed the subject. The woman was a bad liar. "I heard Caitlin loved birds."

"Oh, yes. Cat loved her birds, especially Einstein, the injured great blue that she found along the road. I never saw her without him."

"How could a college student keep a pet great blue?"

"Well, I don't know where she kept it before meeting Tomas, but after meeting him, Einstein was kept out back. They brought Einstein out here that first Saturday. Tomas made a cage out of old wood. It was amazing. That girl would whistle and that bird would come running. He had an injured wing so couldn't fly. I've never seen anything like it."

Obviously, she'd never been a guest in Shark's home.

"Is Einstein there now? I'd love to see him."

"Why no. We haven't seen it since . . . No, he's not."

So, the bird left the trailer, and if it was left to nature is now most likely dead.

"I don't suppose you saw Caitlin the day Tomas, ah, passed? She didn't happen to be in the truck when he came looking for his dad, was she?"

"Oh, no. No, she wasn't."

"And Einstein was in the cage when he left?"

"That was odd. He wasn't. I had planned to tell Tomas when he arrived, but with his fear and all, I didn't."

"Was the cage door latched when you noticed it was missing?"

154

"Yes it was. I assumed Caitlin had come when I was at my neighbors after Tomas left and took him. I can't imagine who else would do that. I remember thinking that Tomas would be happy she was on Pine Island, but I never got the chance to give him the news."

"Any chance Tomas took him?"

"He would never have done that. He was so scared and in no condition to think about Caitlin's bird. Oh . . ." She broke out into sobs. "Why didn't I insist that he stay here? If only I had insisted."

I comforted Mariana, then asked if she minded if I walked out back and looked at the cage. She said she didn't and I left her sitting at the table, reaching for another tissue.

Made out of aged wood, the cage was about five feet tall, seven feet long, and four feet wide. Except for the bottom, all sides were covered in chicken wire. The latch was attached at adult height. I guessed they didn't want their eight-year-old daughter being able to get near the bird without an adult. Made sense to me. I don't trust any beast that can't say "Hey." The latch was locked. A metal plaque of an owl hung over the door. Seeing it made something in the back of my mind creep forward. I waited for it to surface, but nothing did. Give it time, I told myself, and it would.

I left without returning to the house. As I drove down the lane, Shorty's truck lumbered past. I slowed, then stopped as he backed up.

"Any news?"

"Nothing yet. Just paying my respects."

He shot a look toward the house, then back at me. "She okay?" But he didn't wait for an answer.

I pressed the gas pedal and my monkey ring went off. I reached into my breast pocket for my phone and saw it was Hawk.

Caitlin, Hawk informed me, had gone to North Carolina immediately after high school with her brother and her parents. After that, she was taken to the Menninger Clinic in Houston, Texas, where she was under treatment for a year. All particulars confidential. And all details confirmed by credible sources. "In case you don't know, Menninger Clinic is for treatment of mental disorders," he added.

When I re-pocketed the phone, the car bumped along until I reached the stop sign at the Stringfellow intersection. Traffic whizzed past on the two-way highway. Distracted, I thought about Caitlin and her mysterious bird named Einstein, about mental institutions that took patients who wouldn't obey their parents, about illegal term paper scams, about falsely accused gay brothers, and drug trafficking, and untrustworthy FBI agents. Then there was the murder of Dr. Peters and the attempt on my life. It was enough to make me wonder why I just didn't high-tail it back to Cambridge.

The screech of squealing tires made my head snap around. Without thinking, I raised my arms to protect my face as a black pickup out of control bore down on me. Hooded driver. Flash of large sunglasses. I pressed on the gas pedal.

Then … I screamed.

26

"Don't move. Stay still."

The voice was that of Shorty Moore.

I groaned. My head felt as if it had been hit by a sledgehammer. The pain in my arms made me want to vomit. The features of Shorty's face were distorted.

"What happened?" I asked. But I remembered. Black truck. Screeching tires. Hooded driver. I rolled my head to the side.

"Don't do that. Stay still," Shorty insisted, placing his hands on either side of my head. "Ah, there's the ambulance."

"What happened to the other driv . . .?"

My mind went blank.

27

I had two broken arms, three fractured ribs, a concussion, and multiple contusions, but the doctor said I was lucky. Lucky was not how I felt; that is, not until I heard the condition of the driver. Both of my arms were now in plaster casts. The driver was hanging at death's door.

Zen, red-faced and ready for a fight, blew into the room as I was trying to make sense out of what happened. Two officers had just left. I could tell them little. Zen clung to Gar. She was so mad I thought she might grab my IV pole and hit me with it. The level of her anger made her swear like a banshee. When I assured her I was fine, to my relief, she put Gar on the bedside cabinet and her emotional gage seemed to drop a notch.

"Gull dang it, hon. Look at you. Why the hell did you ditch me? This would never have happened if I'd been with you. And you didn't even take your good luck charm along. Fool!"

"Hey, Zen . . . chill. It was a car accident. Accident, get it? You being in the car would only mean you would be in the hospital bed beside me. And, well, not taking Gar—you've got a point there. I'm okay. As far as not taking you along, I wanted to get some information and I was afraid if you were there folks wouldn't speak freely." I tried to raise my hand, but decided against it. "Make sense?"

Zen burst into tears, then in the next second began to laugh and hiccup at the same time. "Guess they got you hogtied now, don't they?" She swiped her nose. "How many shots in the butt did they have to give you? Plenty, I bet."

I stuck my tongue out at her. "I'll be out by tomorrow," I said. Well, I hoped so.

"You redheaded Irish girls don't have the sense you were born with. There ain't no doctor going to let you out in no twenty-four hours. Ain't that a heart monitor you're hooked up to?"

I heard Jay talking to someone in the hallway. "Hey, there should be a comb in that drawer. Get it will you? PLEASE do something about my bangs."

Zen took her sweet time going to the cabinet, but she did have what hair could be seen under control before Jay came into the room.

"Ah!" Jay clutched a bouquet of yellow roses and was followed to my bedside by Chris. Seeing them made my heart beat faster. Chris held a super enormous box. My taste buds began to water.

"Luke sends his love from New York. We couldn't get Gator. He's out on a boat."

Jay's face was pale. "They said you'd had an accident, but oh, I didn't expect this."

"That bad, huh?"

They laughed nervously, then Zen brought me a mirror from the drawer.

The crown of my head was wrapped in a gauze bandage. I was attached to an IV pole and a heart monitor and both eyes were black and blue. Not the picture of health I liked to transmit to the world.

"Bones heal," I mumbled. "Bruises fade."

Jay sat on the side of the bed and I attempted not to show my discomfort with the body movement his action caused.

"Have you heard who the driver was?" I asked.

"Yeah," Jay said. "It was Tomas's girlfriend, Caitlin."

"What?" I tried to sit up straighter, but quickly changed my mind.

"She's in pretty bad shape. Still unconscious. Not sure when she'll come out of it."

I leaned my head back against the pillows. "Was she drunk? The truck seemed out of control."

"It was. Well, might as well tell you. Someone cut her brake lines."

My heart thumped so loud that the heart monitor began making erratic sounds. A nurse rushed in and asked everyone to leave. She gave me two pills. Minutes later I shut my eyes and like a boxer who couldn't get up on count three, I was out.

28

When I opened my eyes, I felt groggy. Zen was sitting in the chair next to the window, playing what I assumed was solitaire on my iPhone. Jay was sitting on the opposite side, reading a magazine. Chris was not in the room. I was no longer hooked up to machines. Head bandages were gone.

It took a few minutes before the objects in the room were clearly visible. The bad print on the wall looked like it was floating in pool water. The chairs Zen and Jay were sitting on appeared covered in feathers. The walls rocked and rolled in rough chop. When Jay moved his head it was the movement of a gopher tortoise. The hospital smell of medicine, cleaning fluids, and sickly patients made my stomach churn. But in my drugged state, I remembered something that had slipped my mind previously.

"Hey, you're awake," Zen said. "Welcome back."

I smiled a weak smile. "You two have nothing better to do than babysit me? Come closer. I want to talk to you so the world in the hallway doesn't overhear."

The metallic sound of their chair legs scraped through my head like chalk on a blackboard. I swallowed hard and counted to ten before being able to speak. My words came out as a hoarse whisper. "Do you guys remember that day in the café when you two convinced me to take this case?"

They nodded.

I cleared my throat. "You had me notice how fearful the customers seemed?"

"Yeah," Jay said.

"So?" Talking was exhausting. I buried my head deeper into my pillow.

Zen and Jay's eyes locked. Jay seemed to take a cue from Zen before he began talking. "Zen, Gator, and I've been discussing that, asking some questions around the islands. Everything leads to concern over drug running."

That's what I thought.

Slowly, I told them my current theory that somehow Caitlin Howard had gotten mixed up with drug dealers. We already knew she participated in illegal acts. It was a hunch, but a heavy-duty one. I also told them that I had a feeling Dr. Sarah Peters had also been involved with the dealing in some way. Maybe she'd found out who was involved, or maybe she was part of the operation but wanted out. I couldn't prove anything yet, but everything seemed to be circling around drugs.

But the skeleton doll, that connection remained a mystery.

As I finished relating my theory, the door swung open. It was Caitlin's parents. After introductions, Jay and Zen excused themselves, saying they'd return after having a cup of coffee in the cafeteria.

I'd forgotten how much Caitlin looked like her mother. Same high cheekbones, long nose, olive-shaped eyes. Her make-up. Her clothes. The way she carried herself. All had a poised, confident air of quality and care. Funny that her daughter's description ran from mousy to lovely, depending upon who she'd spent time with. Was how Caitlin was perceived dependent on how she wanted to be perceived?

I'd also forgotten how handsome Mr. Howard was. I'd heard so many ugly stories about them, I'd put them into a box labeled "demons." I know Grandma, not a smart thing to do. Labeling anyone was never wise, especially for a PI. It thwarted quality logical thinking.

Had the Howards *really* had their daughter institutionalized because she fell in love with a man they didn't approve of? Really?

It was hard to break them out of the "awful" box. And it was difficult to be cordial to them, so I let them begin the conversation. It also didn't help that I had a class-one headache.

"We wanted to see that you're okay," Mrs. Howard said.

I shrugged and as I did, pain shot up from my elbows to my neck. "Peachy keen," I said in a harsh murmur. Then I remembered their daughter's condition. "I'm sorry. That was flip. I heard about Caitlin. I hope, I hope she, ah . . . she's better soon, and that she is totally well again." The words came out as a long sigh.

Mr. Howard, who'd been standing back and to the right of his wife, took a step to the side. "We will never give up hope. But we came for another reason. Robert told us that you're asking questions about Tomas's murder. We have this terrible fear that somehow Caitlin's, ah, accident . . ." He stopped talking and walked closer to the bed. "You've heard that it wasn't an accident?"

I nodded.

"We fear that her attempted murder has something to do with Tomas's death. The police don't think so, but we do."

"You're not asking to hire me I hope, because . . ."

"Oh, no. We plan to hire our own investigator. We're in contact with a true, excuse me, professional."

I know when I've been insulted, but they were right. I'm an amateur. No one knows that better than me. I said nothing, waiting to see how this played out.

"What we are asking is that when he is hired if you would inform him about what you've learned. Anything that would quicken the process of finding this killer is worth it, right?"

This was an interesting turn of events. Did private eyes share information with each other? Intuition said to agree, but logic told me to talk to Hawk about this. I'm drugged after all. One shouldn't make decisions when they're lying in a hospital

163

bed at the mercy of pain-killing meds. I let logic win out and made my eyelids droop lower. "I'm feeling a bit woozy. Would you mind coming back tomorrow? It's been a tough day."

"Oh, of course, my dear. We empathize. We'll be back tomorrow morning. We plan to spend the night with Caitlin."

They were halfway out of the room when I said, "One thing I learned was that Caitlin spent the first year out of high school out of state."

They blanched. Or was that my eyesight playing tricks on me? Mr. Howard took his wife's arm. That was certain. "That's right," he said.

"Could you tell me where she went and why?"

"Why is this important?"

I cleared my throat. The time had come to spill the honest beans. "You said so yourself, I'm investigating the murder of your daughter's boyfriend and now there's been an attempt on her life. I need to gather facts about all involved."

They returned to my bedside. "We assumed you'd found out about that difficult time in our daughter's life. In fact, we were expecting a phone call."

"You were next on my list."

He sighed. "We haven't told anyone about that unfortunate incident."

I bet.

I gave him time to decide how—but I hoped not what— he was going to tell me. In the meantime Mrs. Howard sunk into the chair Zen had vacated. Gar was resting on the table beside her, taking everything in.

"Our daughter has mental issues."

Here we go. Bad parenting excuses.

"Mental issues?"

Mr. Howard continued. "She suffers from manic depression. One day she flies high. The next she can't get off the sofa. It all started her senior year in high school. She was a straight-A student. Everyone says she's brilliant, but she got in with the wrong crowd. We were too overprotective. She

164

rebelled. Two of her, ah, friends talked her into joining them at a night club. Getting fake IDs is as easy as buying toothpaste. They made the mistake of going home with young men they met in the club . . ."

Mrs. Howard grabbed a sob like a catcher snags a spitball.

"Lily, honey, why don't you go back to Caitlin. You don't need to hear this again."

Biting her lip, Mrs. Howard stood, and hanging her head, left the room.

He continued as soon as his wife's footsteps faded. "As a joke, the other girls left while Caitlin was in the bathroom. She was raped. Not by one, but by two of the drunken men. Not once, but multiple times. She wouldn't let us call the police. No charges were ever filed. But Caitlin hasn't been the same since. Afterward, she refused to return to high school. She took her final exams at home and although she was the valedictorian, she did not attend graduation.

Since that night she has lived in a fantasy world, and she often puts herself in situations that will get her into trouble, the more trouble the better it seems." He took a seat. "I'm assuming you found out that she was kicked out of Gulf U for writing and selling term papers for other students?"

I nodded.

His shoulders heaved. "The doctors say it's a reaction to the rape. She feels like she deserves to be punished. No one can make her believe that it wasn't her fault—that she didn't . . . well . . . ask for it."

He shot out of the chair and began to pace. "After she graduated from high school, we had to force her to be committed and we took Robert along thinking he could help her understand the value of getting therapy. Now she hates all three of us. We just don't know what to do anymore."

"Was Tomas aware of any of this?"

Mr. Howard stopped at the foot of my hospital bed. "Something Tomas said alerted me that Caitlin had told him a bizarre story. When I questioned him about it, he confessed that she said she had fallen in love with our gardener and we had had her committed to keep them apart. I told him we'd never had a male gardener under our employ and we would never stand in the way of either of our children following their hearts. He was amazed. I sat him down and told him the truth."

"How did he take it?"

"Just like any man who loved a woman would, with empathy and sorrow."

He tapped the bed frame. "While I'm being honest here, let me clarify something. My son is gay. I didn't know this until recently and I'm afraid I was a bit of a prig when I learned the news. For a while, my foolishness separated us. I believe he got support from a gay professor at the U. I'm thankful for that. After much soul searching, I came to accept my son as a gay man. We had dinner. I apologized. He accepted my apology. We recently had his boyfriend for the weekend. He's a nice guy. I like him." Something made him smile. "His friend kind of reminds me of myself when I was his age." His expression sobered. "Anyway, I hope learning all this helps your investigation in some way and encourages you to work with my investigator to bring this killer to justice.

That night was when I realized that Caitlin was spreading lies about us and about Robert because when Robert came in and introduced his boyfriend, Tomas paled considerably. When I asked him what was wrong, he wouldn't say, but later, after Robert and his beau left, he told me Caitlin had accused her brother of incest. I was livid and after Tomas left, confronted Caitlin with the fiction."

"How did she react?"

"She spit in my face."

29

The next day I was administered fewer pain meds and was more clear-headed. I had plenty of time to review the case and contemplate what I knew. The killer, I surmised, was Caitlin, a woman who could easily have flown into a rage when Tomas rejected her. I was sure of it, but I had no proof.

I asked to be released, but no way would the doctor discharge me. Jay brought me a stack of note cards (Sorry teach. I'll call them what I want.) and a new bouquet of roses—this time white. He was very gentle with me, never pushing, never insisting. I was relieved.

All the while, Zen sat in her chair by the window playing solitaire on my smartphone. Unless another visitor she trusted was present, she refused to leave my bedside.

I picked up the drawing pad Jay had brought, and although the casts made it awkward, began to draw: Caitlin. Tomas. His mom. A great blue. A skeleton doll complete with hat. An owl.

My eyes widened. Wasn't there an owl stamped on that paper that skeleton doll was wrapped in? Oh, yeah, there was. Dr. Peters wore an owl necklace and earrings. Mariana Moore had pictures of owls and figurines of owls in the kitchen, and there was an owl plaque over the bird cage Tomas had built. And didn't Tomas buy owl-shaped candy from CW Fudge for his mom?

I tapped the pencil against the pad and reread my notes. Mariana Moore mentioned she was at the neighbor's house the night Tomas was killed. Caitlin must have been there too.

Okay then. I looked at Zen. "You know who lives in that house on the way to the Moores?"

Zen looked up. "Oh, yeah. That's one scary chick. People say she's into black magic."

The hairs at the base of my skull tingled. The religious cult? She had my full attention. "Yeah?"

"People steer clear of that place."

I tried to recall the house, but I only came up with a shadowy image. I did remember that it was set amongst the palms of an abandoned nursery.

"More. Tell me more."

"Every now and again, people on Stringfellow hear music and chantin`. When I first came to the area, I was looking for the Lazy Flamingo `cause I heard they needed a waitress and I got lost. I made the mistake of knocking on that door." Zen's expression clouded. She tapped the phone against her thigh.

"And?"

"This damn black cat jumped me. I know—a cat—what's the big deal. But this sucker was as big as a small panther. In fact, I ain't sure that it wasn't a panther. I thought it was going to take my face off. When I screamed and fought it off, I know I saw a human in the window. But not a soul came out to help me. I barely made it out of there with my life. You ain't never getting me on that place again."

With Zen's company or without, the first stop when I got out was that house.

Zen went back to her game and I made four lines on my hospital table with my cards. Read each one. Shuffled them around. Read them again. Trying to figure out what else I'd missed.

30

Zen was in the bathroom. I sat in her chair, waiting for her to carry my suitcase. It was ten a.m., May 15th and I'd been discharged. Someone tapped on the door.

"Come in," I said, expecting it to be Jay. I hated to admit it to myself, but I liked all the flowers and missed him after he left.

Zen came out of the bathroom as Mr. Howard walked in.

"Ms. Murphy, could you please come to our daughter's room? She came to and wants to talk to you."

Caitlin was lying perfectly still when our entourage entered. Her brother stood on her left, and her mother sat in a chair on her right, holding her hand.

Mr. Howard stepped to her side. "I've brought Ms. Murphy, dear."

Caitlin's head rolled to the side.

"No, no. Lie still. Here she is." He made room for me at her bedside.

Caitlin mumbled something to her mother who patted her hand and stood. "She wants to be alone with Ms. Murphy."

Everyone, including my devoted watchdog, Zen, left the room.

I looked down at Caitlin.

"You look terrible," she said.

"Yeah, well, I'm being discharged. This will all heal."

"I guess."

We gazed into each other's eyes for quite some time then Caitlin looked away. "I was really angry with you, you know."

"Why?"

"For believing me."

"Really?"

"I thought you'd see through my lies. Punish me. Get me recommitted."

"I, uh . . ."

She interrupted me. "Crazy, huh? To want to be punished. That's what everyone keeps telling me."

"Seems normal to me."

"It does?"

"Sure. You went to a nightclub. Probably wore clothes you normally don't wear. Flirted with some guys. Got tipsy. Made the mistake of going home with them."

"But that didn't mean I wanted them to rape me!" she almost screamed.

"Exactly," I said quietly.

Our eyes locked again. I sat on the side of the bed. "So, do you want to tell me the truth?"

Her chest rose and fell. She closed her eyes. Her lips formed a thin line. She turned her head, mumbling a word I didn't catch. I asked her to repeat it.

"Yes," she whispered, "yes."

I waited.

"I killed Tomas," she confessed.

There it was.

"Just like I've been destroying Robert and my parents." She stared at the ceiling. "He was such a nice guy. So gullible. So easy to fool." Her eyes caught mine. "Most people believe you, you know, when they think you're weak and vulnerable."

In my mind I raised my hand.

She continued, "I'm not weak. I'm tough. Big Joe figured that out right away. I'm tougher and sneakier than anyone could ever guess."

I didn't know what to say. The casts on my arms were uncomfortable. I needed somewhere to rest them. I rolled over the hospital table.

"I wanted Tomas to beat up my brother. To make him pay for agreeing I needed to get professional help. I wanted him to spit on my folks—to show them his scorn."

She closed her eyes again, then smiled a sad smile. "But he was smarter than I thought. Turned out he believed them, not me. Go to hell, I told him." She made a phiff noise. "The fool. He said he still loved me. That he would stick with me through everything." She caught a sob. "Can you believe it? He knew I was a liar and he still loved me?"

A cloud drifted over the sun in my brain.

"That night when he called me at Big Joe's, I'd brought a surprise. Tomas was so driven to get a degree with honors, he was so careful not to do anything that would get him in trouble. He never even drank more than one beer." She ran her hand through her hair, then continued. "I was going to show him how it felt to have your whole world turned upside down by one mistake." Her eyes clamped shut again and remained closed so long I became concerned.

"I'll get the nurse."

Her eyes popped open. "No! I need to finish this."

"Okay," I said in a soft voice.

"I bought some cocaine at the U. It's easy to get. Everyone knows the source. My plan was to convince him to come back to the dorm with me and I'd get him to sniff some coke and call the TA. Even if he didn't sniff it, I'd have it visible so when the TA got into my room we'd both be caught in possession. That would fix him for good.

Tomas was in his trailer. He was uneasy, panicky. He wouldn't tell me why. He kept looking out the windows. He was angry I'd brought Einstein along and was talking crazy stuff. He wouldn't think of coming back to the dorm with me. Said that was dangerous. He said we should leave Florida and start a new life together far away. He said we'd have to drop Einstein off at his parents' house. We'd have to send for him later. I couldn't do that, I told him. But he wouldn't listen. I'd brought a couple of beers and we drank them while he talked. He made me so nervous, I did a stupid thing. I brought out the coke and he went ballistic. "Where did you get it? Where?" he kept screaming. He stood up and began pushing me out the door. I struggled, telling him I wanted Einstein, but I couldn't find him. When we went outside looking for him, a car drove up. Tomas pushed me into my truck and said to get out of there. He promised he'd bring Einstein to me in the morning.

I was halfway down the drive when I realized I'd left the cocaine in the trailer. I should have gone back. If I had, he wouldn't have been murdered." She began to sob. "By not returning I killed him."

I remained sitting on the bed until her sobs subsided. What a sad young woman. How could anyone not feel sorry for her? How positive I had been that she was the killer. When she was under control I assured her that she most likely would only have been killed herself if she'd returned.

"Did you tell Tomas who you bought your coke from?"

"Yeah."

"And who was that?"

She refused to look at me. "I'm not saying."

"Why?"

"That's probably who killed Tomas. Maybe he called and threatened them with going to the police after I left. He was mad enough. Maybe they came and killed him. Maybe if I tell, I'll be the next victim."

Good deduction I was thinking. Could I blame her? I'd probably do the same in her shoes. Not that I could afford her shoes.

"What were you doing at the neighbor's house the night of our accident?" I asked.

"Looking for Einstein, but a big cat hissed at me and I left."

"So what was your plan to get even with me?" I asked.

She looked away.

That's when it hit me. My voice was a whisper wrapped in a thin sheet of horror. "*You* shot at me from a boat and when that didn't work, you cut your brake lines and aimed for my car? You tried to kill us both?"

Mr. Howard was leaning against the hallway wall with his arm around his weeping wife. Robert, not far from Zen, stood nearby, a horrified look on his face.

"She actually said she'd cut the line herself?"

"She did."

Mr. Howard pulled his wife closer. "And you'll press charges?"

"The police," I said, "will need to know about the suicide attempt."

"Of course."

"And Caitlin will get professional help again. I don't see what good filing charges would do. By telling outrageous lies, Caitlin was begging for help. She knew she shouldn't have been released from the mental institution."

Okay, Grandma, so I was forgiving her attempting to kill me twice. Whatever. She wasn't successful, right?

Zen and I returned to the room, leaving the Howards to their grief. My suitcase, Gar and the two bouquets of roses were stacked on a handy cart.

Although I realized that no one at the Moores' neighbor had cut Caitlin's brake line. I was more than curious about who lived in that house. Perhaps whoever lived there was the source of the drugs. I wanted to meet that neighbor. The words "owl," "drugs," and "skeleton doll" circled through my head. "Take me to Pine Island," I said as we exited the hospital.

"Shouldn't you be restin` or something?" Zen asked.

"I may not be able to drive, but my brain still works. I want to go to that house near the Moores."

"The haunted one?"

"Haunted?"

"That's what plenty say."

"That's the one."

"Holy Jesus, MOTHER OF GOD!" Zen's eyes were the size of quarters.

So much for a fearless partner in crime.

31

It was high noon when Zen turned left onto the driveway leading through the overgrown palm farm. I ducked when a black cormorant flew too close to the windshield.

Zen swore. "At least it's day time," she muttered.

We pulled up in front of the mobile home. The porch was disconnected from the house. No one had tended the trees or yard in years.

"Keep your eyes out for that panther," Zen warned. "I can't believe you got me here."

We left the car and with each step, Zen became more and more agitated. Unfortunately, her anxiety was contagious. By the time we got close to the door and I saw the rusted metal plate engraved with an owl, I needed a Valium. Zen needed three.

Straightening my shoulders, I knocked firmly. Zen's head did not stop rotating as she kept lookout for the attacking cat.

No response. I knocked again. The sound of breaking glass made me jump as Zen nudged herself closer to me, knocking me slightly off balance. I drew in my breath, widened my stance and waited.

The door squeaked open, but no one was visible.

I looked at Zen. She looked at me. The door opened another inch.

"Let's get out of here," Zen mouthed.

A musty stench from the dim interior of the house enveloped us. I crinkled my nose. The door creaked again.

Praying to the Universe I wasn't making a mistake, I stepped inside and I'm sure because her desire to protect me was stronger than her fear, Zen tiptoed in as well.

Although the room was cast in shadow, I made out stacks of clutter everywhere I looked. Something crawled across my foot. "Eww."

"What!?"

"Something ran across my toes."

The door swung shut with a snap that rattled the walls.

"Shit!"

Slowly, like two wide-eyed kids at a house of horror, we turned.

A woman with graying black hair draping her shoulders faced us. A floor-length brightly colored dress covered her six-foot frame. A large owl pendant hung from the gold braid around her waist. Pointed sleeves covered her hands. The word priestess came to my mind. So did Tomas's funeral. This was the woman I'd noticed at in the church, the one I presumed to be a psychic, but never had seen again. Hadn't there been another, younger woman with her? One, because of the close resemblance, I assumed was her daughter? I wondered where she was.

I fumbled with introductions. Her name was Daniela Diaz. She apologized for the dim light. Said her eyes were sensitive. All but floating past us, she led us into a small kitchen. I was thinking what a good actress she was. I'm sure I'd seen this scene on stage.

As my eyes adjusted to the lack of artificial or natural light, I saw that what I had first thought was clutter, wasn't clutter at all, but signs of packing.

"You're moving?"

Daniela settled in a chair and motioned for us to sit. "Yes. I'm moving in with my daughter. She's having a difficult time adjusting to the death of her sister. She was murdered recently at Gulf Coast University by some maniac."

"Your daughter was Sarah Peters?" I asked.

"You knew her?"

"Not really. I spoke to her only once. I'm so sorry for your loss."

She lowered her head. "Have you come for a reading?" she asked.

A reading? She actually *was* a psychic?

"Yes," I lied. Well, I had past acting experience too. Like, one course in college that I almost failed. "My friend brought me since right now I can't drive." As if I didn't think she'd get it, I held up my pathetic arms that were weighted down by the white casts. I didn't believe in psychics—but Grandma Murphy swore by them and in my eyes Grandma had the power of the Pope. It would be so much fun to tell her about this experience. She would be so very impressed that I'd had a reading. Of course I wouldn't tell her that it wasn't planned. She didn't need to know everything.

Daniela looked at Zen, then at me. "I don't usually read so an observer can hear." She gazed steadily at Zen. "Do you mind waiting in the other room?"

Zen's facial muscles tightened. "I'll stay right here," she said.

The woman showed no change in expression, but she turned to me. "You don't mind? Readings are often quite personal."

"Nah. She's my bud. We share everything."

Nodding, she rested her arms on the table, palms up. "If it doesn't make you uncomfortable, put your hands over mine."

Truth was—it did make me jittery, but I swallowed my discomfort. As our flesh touched, her eyes closed.

Zen gave me a disgusted look. I winked at her, but the act of bravado was false. My big toe was keeping time to a Michael Jackson tune.

"Your accident was no accident," the woman said in a hushed voice.

My eyes widened. Had she witnessed it? Seen Caitlin cutting her own brakes?

177

"I see an older woman standing close to you—a mother, an aunt—no, a grandmother. Danger surrounds us . . . you." Her chest rose and fell. "You feel guilt. You lost a loved one, but he wants you to move on. To be happy."

Okay, so that was a bit too close to home. Maybe Grandma was right, psychics did have special insight. Well . . . maybe. . .

For several seconds, Daniela did not speak. Then she said, "You're searching for something . . . no someone."

Silence again. Her eyes opened. She withdrew her hands.

The air in the room had evaporated. Zen's eyes were wide. The woman placed one hand over the other in front of her chin and gazed steadily at me.

A car door slammed.

Zen started. I motioned for her to remain quiet.

"Oh, thank you. That was so helpful. I'm sure the danger has to do with the sea. I was thinking of going diving. You can bet I'm canceling that trip tonight. And searching? You bet. I'm searching for a new man for my grandma. She lost my grandpa a few years back and she's so lonely. Your reading was amazing really. I must do this again. When are you leaving here? Where can I find you after you move?"

Daniela told us she was leaving in two days and she willingly gave me her daughter's address. She asked if Zen wished a reading. When Zen said no, she said I could put the fifty dollars in the basket on the counter.

Fifty bucks! Crapola!

Standing, we said goodbye. I took a good look at a box near the door as I fished out fifty bucks and placed it in the basket before going outside.

"Hey, did you see that?" I asked.

"What?"

"Two people just headed down that path."

"Probably just workers."

"Workers?" I repeated. No way.

"Maybe they're clearing the land. This is a prime building site."

"Are you kiddin`?"

But I dropped the subject momentarily. I was distracted, thinking of what just happened in the trailer. Here was the connection I was looking for. Dr. Peters was this woman's daughter. The doctor daughter could have been the campus distributor. And the other daughter? That piece of the puzzle was still to be fit in place. But at least the image of the puzzle was visible.

I cocked my head. "You hear that?"

Zen nudged closer to me. "Sounds like chantin` or cats." She pushed me toward the car. "Come on. We're out of here."

As she backed out of the drive, the curtain in the living room lowered and I knew we would be returning.

32

"What's this have to do with Tomas's death?" Zen asked, then swore as the car hit a pothole.

Pain shot up my arms. I yelped.

"Sorry," she said.

I told her what I was thinking, that this isolated woman could have been supplying drugs to her daughter who was then selling it to her students. "Plus," I said, "Tomas's adviser, his mom, and this woman all wear the same owl symbol. That same symbol was stamped on the paper Tomas wrapped the doll in. I think that's more than a coincidence."

"Hm, interesting," Zen said, "You think Tomas's mom gets psychic readings from Daniela?"

"Quite possibly. I think we should see what's going on behind that trailer. And we can't just park in front of the house and stroll down there like two tourists. Got any ideas?"

"But that would mean we walk through that overgrown palm farm. Do you know how many snakes are on Pine Island? Shit!"

"We'll wear rubber boots."

"Sure we will. Damn." Zen switched on the radio, turning up the volume. I rolled down the window.

At the only four-way stop on Pine Island, Zen pushed in the radio "Off" button. "Mariana seems the vulnerable type."

"Yeah, maybe Mariana was going through too much money for readings—and Tomas found out about it."

"Maybe Tomas went to that woman and told her to lay off his mom," Zen added.

"And perhaps Daniela's involved with the drug runners and they didn't like Tomas snooping around."

"And we know what happened to Tomas," Zen said. "If we're right, we damn well know they won't like us snoopin` around either."

I said nothing.

"Didn't she say you were surrounded by danger?"

"She did."

"Do you remember what I told you about her attacker cat?"

"Yep."

"You an airhead, or what?"

"I've been called worse."

33

Jay had invited Zen and me for dinner, but Zen said she'd take a raincheck. Of course she would. I had three hours before I had to get ready, so I phoned Hawk and gave him Daniela Diaz's name. After this, I drove to the library and spent an hour or so surfing the web.

Jay had made a peach pie to celebrate my release from the hospital. The table was set with a single rose in the middle.

"I picked up crab legs at the fish house. Potatoes are in the oven. Salad is ready to be tossed." He handed me a glass of Chablis. We smiled at each other. "Welcome home," he said and we touched glasses.

All through the meal I thought about the psychic reading. I really didn't believe in psychics, but Daniela's words had been more than astute. The accident had not been an accident. I most likely was in danger. After all, I was investigating a murder case and getting darn close to catching a killer. And guilt had been a compelling force in my life. Less than a year ago the man I thought of as my soulmate had been murdered in Matlacha. I felt guilty that I had let him come to Florida without me. After I found his killer, every time I saw a man I was attracted to, I felt guilty. Sleeping with Jay made that beast gnaw at me like a shark gnaws on defenseless flesh.

Daniela seemed to have channeled Will's spirit. I most definitely believed in an afterlife. He wants you to be happy, she'd said. I stepped toward Jay. He set down his glass and encircled me in his strong arms.

Let me be able to let go, I told myself. Let me be able to move on.

Because of the awkward casts, because I was preoccupied with the case, I was sure Jay would be ready to end it all.

But he wasn't. And I wasn't. As in, no way.

Later, as in . . . much later, when Jay took me home I felt rejuvenated, ready to wrap up this case so I could get back home to start cleaning my apartment in Cambridge. Jay planned to visit in June.

34

The following night Zen helped me pull rubber boots over my jeans, which was next to impossible for me to do with my arms in casts. The boots came from Gator. He'd asked why we wanted them and Zen gave a lame excuse, something about wading out searching for shells. Gator was pissed that he wasn't invited to join us, but we didn't have time to explain.

Zen wore a pair of overalls and a forest-green cap. We both had chosen long-sleeved shirts and doused ourselves generously with Skin So Soft.

The plan was to park in a spot that Zen knew about that abutted the palm farm near the sea. She was confident that there was only one clearing. She'd once explored the farmland with an archaeological group.

I had contemplated ditching Zen and doing this solo, but even if I managed to get away from her, she'd know where I was. Best to stick together. I insisted we take Gar along. Zen protested.

"I won't take him out of the car," I insisted, "but he's good luck. We may need him."

Zen agreed luck was a necessity on this mission. I suspected the cat/panther, poisonous snakes, wild pigs, and no-see-ums were her major concerns. Mine was the possibility of having drug dealers catching us spying on them.

I sent a prayer for safety to the Universe while Zen continually swore under her breath as we made our way through the hiker-unfriendly terrain.

I'd brought along my camera, a flashlight in case we got lost on the return trek, and two bottles of water. It was still light out, but wouldn't be for long. I stopped and pulled out the plastic containers. Zen took one and held up a first-aid kit. "For snake bites," she said.

Much of the land was swampy. Our boots sunk into the mush and made a "whup" sound when we pulled them out. After a while, I had to admit, I wondered what kind of snakes liked water and lived on the island. I shoved up the bill of my cap and glanced at Zen. On high alert, her head moved constantly as she struggled forward.

I took another step, then stopped. Human footfalls. Zen hesitated and looked at me. I put my finger to my lips. "Shh."

Hunkering down, I signaled Zen to follow suit.

The sound of walking feet became louder.

I ducked behind a bushy pygmy palm and she joined me. A clearing was five feet away. Several people stood without talking, hands folded in front of them. I pulled the camera strap from around my neck and began clicking. Zen nudged me with her elbow and nodded toward the right. Daniela, in a long white dress with a hood, entered the clearing. She was followed by the familiar younger woman who resembled Sarah Peters and who also was dressed in flowing white. I clicked again. They walked slowly toward us, then turned their backs and stopping in front of a boulder, faced the center. There appeared to be a scarecrow-like object near the rock.

Others entered the clearing. I recognized no one amongst the twenty or so people.

Click. Click.

Then, head down, Mariana Moore in a head scarf, took a place.

Click.

No one spoke. No one milled around.

The silence was unnerving. I feared Zen would whisper or lose her cool. A twig snapped. Our heads swiveled and we watched an armadillo slide into the underbrush. I grimaced at Zen. She gave me the same look.

We returned our attention to the activity in the clearing. Daniela and the other woman dressed in white slipped their hoods over their long hair and the group began to pray. At first, the Spanish words were a low hum, but slowly the hum intensified and became the disconcerting buzz of a million bees. The noise could easily be mistaken for chanting.

Zen put her hands over her ears. I continued to take pictures.

Daniela raised her arms and everyone silenced. She and the younger woman sat on the boulder near the scarecrow which I now realized wasn't a scarecrow at all, but a life-sized skeleton doll.

One by one individuals walked forward, holding objects or an envelope. With bowed heads, they placed them on the boulder and returned to their place, some in tears, all solemn.

Zen and I gave each other a "Whoa!" look.

Once the last person returned to their place, another praying session began. Then led by Daniela and flanked by the younger woman, who first hesitated at the statue, everyone disappeared into the bowels of the abandoned palm farm.

"What was that?" Zen whispered.

"Shh, wait until they're farther away. I want to see that statue."

While Zen kept her eye out for cat/panthers, snakes, or wild boar—human or otherwise, I scanned through the photos I'd taken. One figure at the back of the group who had not gone to the boulder looked familiar, but I wasn't sure. I found the shot and zoomed in. As I suspected, the person under the hooded sweatshirt was Ty Chambers, Tomas`s college roommate. I pocketed the phone and we crept forward.

The mega-doll was . . . eww . . . a real skeleton tied to a pole. It was dressed as a woman in colorful clothes and a flower-adorned hat. She was holding a scythe and a globe.

Here was a bigger version of the skeleton doll—what I had learned was Santa Muerta, Saint Death, a fallen angel of mythical proportions worshiped by many in Mexico and now also in the states. The macabre figure was surrounded by offerings: packs of cigarettes, flowers, fruit, incense, alcoholic beverages, candles, and plastic-wrapped candy. I noticed the envelopes were gone. I assumed they were filled with cash. The more heartfelt the desired outcome the more given. But what were they asking for?

Zen eyed the skeleton. "Jesus! Is that real?"

"Afraid so. Remind you of anything?"

Zen squeezed her expression into a weird mask-like shape. Under the moonlight, she appeared frightened, fitting for our situation.

"That doll Tomas left for you. Right?"

I gave a quick nod and pointed. "And look at the painting on that boulder."

"An owl?"

"Yeah, and there was an owl stamped on the white paper the doll was wrapped in. According to what I read, the owl serves as one of their symbols. Santa Muerta is supposed to be powerful, mysteriously granting many favors, especially to criminals."

"Criminals?"

"Yeah. Authorities have linked the worship of Santa Muerta to prostitution, drug trafficking, kidnapping, smuggling, and even homicides. The practice was always pretty secretive. This must be a local place of worship."

"And Tomas's mom is involved with this?"

"Yeah. Scary, huh?"

"What if Tomas found out about it and demanded she stop? A criminal found out about how her offerings would dry up and took care of the problem?"

"Good God!"

"Come on, let's get out of here."

As usual Bert's was jiving. Zen and I sat at the bar, Guinness and Bud in hand. Live soul-touching music performed its magic inside and outside of the building. Blue grass in the back room. Jamaican near the front of the outside seating area. The TV was on. Customers were in high vocal spirits. A pool ball slammed into a pocket. A woman laughed. One of the front doors opened and closed. I took another sip of my beer. Neither Zen nor I had yet brought up what we had just witnessed. Apparently, like me, she needed some process time. The bartender asked if we wanted another beer. We shook our heads in unison. Zen started up a conversation with a man on her left. Another man came our way from the back room. He looked familiar. Our eyes caught briefly and he stopped at my side.

"Hi, remember me?"

I lowered my gaze.

Tobin Peterson, the Lee County deputy who was friends with Tomas, raised his glass and smiled into my eyes. "Want to catch a movie some night?"

My neck muscles immediately stiffened. "Oh, well, sorry. I'm involved right now. Thanks for asking though."

"No harm in trying, right?"

I kept my eye roll to myself. "So no interest in helping find your fishing buddy's killer? I haven't seen you or the sheriff around."

Peterson's expression went solemn. "We're working on it."

"Mum's the word, right?"

"It's police business. I'm not . . ."

"Yeah. Yeah. Yeah."

He raised his glass and backed away.

Zen, who had glanced a couple of times at Peterson while we briefly talked, swiveled to face me. "Since when are you friendly with Tobin Peterson?"

"I'm not," I said.

"The look in his eyes tells a different story," Zen said, taking a long swig of beer.

I looked behind me to see if I could see him. He was standing near a window. Our eyes caught again and he raised his glass. I looked away.

"He's not my type. He'll get over it."

"You didn't tell him anything about what we've discovered, did you?"

"You kiddin`?"

"Just checkin`. I don't think the Moores are interested in the cops, if you know what I mean."

I did. No one in the area seemed to trust them.

"So, what was your take on the Pine Island drama?" Zen asked.

Good question. What *did* I think of what we had just witnessed? I went for humorous.

"Hooded dresses were a nice touch," I said. "Very Hollywood."

Zen's expression went solemn. "I knew a gal once—she got caught up in a group like that. Brainwashed. Couldn't make a decision without consulting the leader. Sick. Real sick."

"How'd she break away?"

"Parents kidnapped her, then hired a counselor to reprogram her. Took years."

I thought about Mariana Moore, wondering how long she'd been involved with this worship practice. Wondered how deep she was into it, how much money she'd donated.

"Have you ever heard anyone mention this type of activity going on in Pine Island?"

"Just the stuff about hearin` chantin` and rumors the place was haunted. Nothin` else. Course I'm not tight with the local religious crowd."

"Why didn't you mention this before? Didn't it occur to you that maybe this is why everyone is nervous? They don't get what's going on. Lack of understanding breeds fear. God, Zen, did you never connect the skeleton doll to this religious crowd as you call it?"

189

"Hey, cool it. No I didn't. I ain't no genius. If I had, don't you think I would of mentioned it?"

This was the first time I'd seen Zen pout. She was actually quite cute when she pouted. I had to smile and pat her on the shoulder.

"Sorry. This case has me on edge. Or maybe it's all the hocus pocus that's doing that. We've made the connection now, that's what's important, right?"

Zen looked at me out of the corner of her eye. "Sure, I suppose."

"Ah, come on. Don't be angry. So I'm a prig sometimes. Call me human."

Of course Zen grinned. She wasn't someone to hold a grudge.

I leaned my head close to hers in a conspirator's sort of way. "Okay, Click, we need to keep this to ourselves. It may be necessary to observe one more time—get ourselves situated where we aren't behind the priestess."

"I was afraid you'd say that. Hey, you know what?"

"What?"

"That's the first time I ever laid eyes on an armadillo in the wild. Pretty cool, huh?"

"Yeah, pretty cool."

We took long swallows of our beers.

"I need to do some research," I said.

"About?"

"The Moores' finances. Did you see that envelope Mariana handed over? It bulged." I also wanted to know more about Ty Chambers, but I kept that information to myself. Zen did not need to know all the details of my investigation.

"Hey, you can't get bank records or charge card statements, can you?" Zen put her hand up to order another Bud.

"I can't. But I know someone who can."

Zen thanked the bartender, picked up her beer and gave me a broad smile. "Remind me to never make you an enemy."

I winked at her and finished my Guinness.

Besides wanting to know about Mariana's finances, I wondered how the fed's drug investigation was going.

When Zen and I returned to Jay's, I phoned Hawk and asked if he could help me out with a financial report on the Moores and Ty Chambers and if he could push harder for information about the local drug investigation and on Daniela Diaz.

Hawk said, "I get answers to these questions, you'll owe me big. You know that, right?"

I assured him I did.

"June 20th. Don't forget. A kid never forgets when his godmother misses a birthday party when she says she'll be there. Be careful, Jess. We love ya."

35

The next day I sat on the sofa gazing at my note cards spread out across the floor.

Zen was on the dock—feet on one of Gator's crab traps—taking in some rays.

"Want to go for a drive?" I yelled.

"Thought you'd never ask. Where to?"

"Gulf U. But don't rush. I need to make a call. I tapped in Ty Chambers` number. He would be happy to meet at two. Zen and I had just had lunch. Perfect, I assured him.

I was interested in asking him a few more questions and in seeing how Tomas and he lived—not that dorm rooms weren't basically the same everywhere—but one never knew what stories a living space had to tell.

We met in the lobby.

"Looks like you got hit by a truck," Ty said.

"I did."

"Ouch. Not fun."

I shrugged. "I'll be back to normal soon."

He greeted Zen and then guided us to the elevator. "The room's all mine until next term," he said, "but I sure wish Tomas's folks would pick up his stuff."

Tomas left stuff the cops didn't take? Cool.

I spoke in a casual tone. "No, problem. We'll take it back to them. Right, Zen?"

"Sure. How come the cops didn't take it?"

The elevator door opened and he ushered us out. "They took most everything, but these are just his clothes. Guess they didn't want them."

We followed him. "It's only two boxes, but I admit, it feels creepy having them here." He left the closet door ajar and turned to Zen. "Is Zen your real name?"

Her eyebrows furrowed. "Why?"

"It's such a cool name." He looked at me. "Don't you think?"

"Nickname," Zen offered.

"Still cool."

They smiled at each other.

"I assume this was Tomas's bed?" I asked.

"Yep." He pointed to the desk that was now lined with various brands of unopened soda bottles.

"And that was his desk. No alcohol allowed in the rooms I presume?" I asked.

"No way. Strict rules on that."

"You ever get out to Pine Island?" I asked.

"Not since the funeral."

Liar. Liar. College boy liar.

Ignoring me, he moved toward Zen. They began to talk. I sat on the edge of Tomas's bed. "Tomas ever say anything to you about needing money?"

He drug his eyes off Zen. "You mean, Mr. Workaholic? He didn't have to say anything. It was obvious. Why else would he hold down three jobs at once while studying his butt off?" He went to his bed and sat, patting the mattress to offer Zen a seat. She walked over and settled real close beside him—their shoulders only inches from touching. "I never could figure him out. He was on a full scholarship," he said, smiling at Zen.

That, I didn't know.

"Did his folks ever visit here?" I asked.

"His dad came once. Seemed like a nice guy. Salt of the earth." He cut a sly look toward Zen. "I've always admired that type."

So Shorty Moore *had* met Ty.

Zen blinked and blinked. I just barely kept from rolling my eyes.

He continued. "They didn't hang around. Tomas was surprised when he showed up and they took off right away. I stepped out in the hall as they left and Tomas's dad was reading him the riot act. Folks? What can you do?" he said, looking directly into Zen's eyes.

"Tomas didn't tell you why his dad was upset with him?"

"Subject never came up."

"Ever meet his mom?"

"Only briefly at the funeral."

I stood. "Would you mind helping Zen carry these boxes to the car? I'll catch up with you. I need to use the john."

They beamed at each other.

I fumbled around in my bag—biding my time—until Zen and Ty picked up the boxes and chatting away, walked out the door. It didn't get past me that my welfare had slipped Zen's consciousness. Such is the power of first attraction.

I waited until I heard the elevator open and close and then shut the door. I began searching first Tomas's desk, under his blotter, then his dresser drawer. Nothing. I glanced right to left. Got down on my hands (awkward with the casts) and knees and inspected under Tomas's bed. Four pairs of shoes. Nothing else. I stood and looked under Ty's bed and found a shoe box. I pulled it out, opened it and stared down at two rows, two deep of plastic bags containing white powder. One tiny touch of it to my lips told me it was cocaine. This was not something the cops would have missed. No way. I slid the box back under the bed.

Why, Mr. Chambers. I do believe you're a salesman. I frowned. Or are you?

Something was off here. Something rather important.

After saying our farewells to Ty, Zen and I (me deep in thought) walked to the car.

"He's kind of nice," Zen mumbled.

"Oh, sure he is. Keep your head about you, girl."

"I know, but . . . still . . . he's kind of nice."

I kept my find to myself for the time being.

36

Back in my room, Zen brought in the two boxes. "I thought these belonged to Tomas's folks," she said.

"Don't worry. They'll get them. Right after we seal them back up again."

Zen's eyes twinkled. I could tell she loved anything on the edge of illegal. She went to a drawer and took out a knife. "Which one first?"

She unsealed one box, which was packed full. Searching pockets, we pulled each item out. "Whoa, look at this!" I held up two paper-clipped statements that had been folded four times.

Zen dropped a shirt and leaned in close. "Charge card bills? Eww. Almost a thirty thou balance. That's even higher than mine."

"Look at the name and address."

"Mariana's name. Tomas's address. Whoops. Not good."

"Yeah, looks like mom was trying to hide something from pop."

"Poor Tomas. Can you imagine being caught in the middle?"

"Take a look at the statement. A three thousand dollar payment was made last month."

"That's a pretty hefty payment for one month," Zen said.

"Yeah. Wonder where she got the money?"

"Her son?"

"Most likely."

Zen looked at me. "You suppose pop found out about this and chewed out Tomas for helping his mom hide her secret?"

"Could be."

"Time to talk to the folks?"

"Oh, yeah."

37

The Moores' dog loped toward the car, causing me a moment's pause, but halfway to us, it stopped to take a dump and my shoulders relaxed. I hadn't phoned. I wanted the element of surprise on my side.

Zen parked under a royal palm. Stepping out of the car, she went to the trunk, taking out one of the boxes. "What if they're both home?"

I'd thought of that possible scenario, but hadn't figured out how I'd handle it yet. "I'm playing this by ear. Listen, do me a favor, don't talk, and leave the other box there for now."

She gave me a puzzled look. "Check. But the boxes aren't heavy, I can carry them both."

"Just do as I say."

She closed the trunk and glanced at the red kid's backpack I'd found at a local thrift store on one of my routine stops. "Want me to carry that?"

"Nope."

I knocked on the door. I'd stopped taking my pain pills and my arms ached.

Shorty, his head covered in a red paisley bandana, opened the door. "Ms. Murphy." He looked at my arm casts and lowered his gaze. "Zen. Come in." He stepped back.

"Mariana at home?" I asked.

"Nah. She's at the neighbor's."

I looked at Zen and our eyes locked.

"How's the body doin`?" Shorty asked. He had come to the hospital twice to see me, but Mariana had not. Shorty said she was watching their daughter.

"Healin`."

"And the driver?"

I couldn't help but notice that he refused to use Caitlin's name.

"I, ah," I said, "am sure she'll get the help she needs."

Zen shot a look at me. I lowered my eyelids with a warning for her to paint her lips shut. It wasn't up to me to spread the sad news that Caitlin had attempted suicide while she tried to do away with me.

"A couple boxes of clothes were left at the U. We brought them to you."

Zen all but dropped the box on the floor near the table. I gave her a tough Murphy look. She shrugged her shoulders and I turned toward Shorty. "I have a few questions. Do you mind?"

"Nah, have a seat."

I sat across from him and nudged my open backpack near the box. "It's about your finances."

He grimaced. "What's my finances have to do with Tomas's death?"

"Maybe nothing. But I have to fill in some holes in my investigation."

He studied the table. "Don't like people to know my business," he muttered, "but go ahead."

"Apparently you didn't know that Tomas was working for Russ Beadle."

"He was not!" Shorty's shoulders rounded. "He was?"

"Since he was fifteen or thereabouts."

"But he was working as a kayak tour guide. When would he have time for his book learnin`?"

"And occasionally hiring on as a fishing guide," I added.

"But he was on a full scholarship. Why did he need the extra money?"

"That's why I'm here."

Shorty ran his hands through his thinning hair. "I had no idea. Three jobs? He never let on."

"Maybe he had extra expenses?"

"Like what? His tuition and housing was paid. He didn't even have to buy his food. His Harley was a gift from my bro. The truck was paid for long ago. For clothes? What does it cost to buy a couple pair of shorts, jeans, and sandals? Besides, he also had a college fund we started when he was a little kid. He used that for extra needs."

"Maybe he was helping out a friend or . . . someone in the family?"

His eyebrows furrowed. "Only friend I knew he had in college was that Howard girl and she's from money, right? In high school, he hung around with one kid, but he was killed last year in a boating accident. And family? Mariana and I have no debt. We don't even have a charge card. I don't trust those things. If someone in the family needed money, they'd come to me, not him. He was a kid. Who takes money from a kid?"

So he didn't know about his wife's debt.

"I understand you went to see Tomas at college."

"Sure, why?"

"His roommate said there had been a confrontation."

Shorty's eyes narrowed, hardened, then teared up. "I should have mentioned that I suppose. It was about the Howard girl. She was wrong for him. He just wouldn't get it. He wouldn't drop her. Nothin' I said made a difference. He was such a damn good kid."

The front door opened and Mariana stepped into the room. Seeing her husband's stricken face, she blanched. "What's wrong?" She hurried to his side.

"Jessie says Tomas needed extra money to help out someone. You know anyone who might of asked Tomas for help?"

Mariana looked from me to Zen to Shorty, then dropped her gaze. "That's silly. Tomas was a college student. He didn't have extra money."

I had the incriminating statements in my bag. Would she confess? Or would I have to force her to?

Shorty related Tomas's work history to his wife. Her eyes grew wider and wider as he talked.

"I . . ." she said. "Oh, dear."

"And you have no idea why he needed the money?" I asked.

"Why . . . I . . ."

There was a time when I would have been too nice to do what I did next, but remembering that Grandma Murphy used to warn me that being too nice was some women's failing, I reached into my bag, pulled out the statements, and placed them on the table.

Shorty looked puzzled. Mariana paled.

"Look at them," I said.

Shorty picked up the papers and scanned them. His cheeks reddened. "Mariana!"

She jumped up from her chair and backed toward the wall. Her face ashen. Her eyes searching everywhere. A caged animal expecting its hunter at her doorstep.

I stood. "We'll go get the other box." I motioned to Zen.

After we stepped off the porch, Zen whispered, "Don't you want to hear them? What kind of PI would let them be alone now?"

"She'll be more honest without us there," I said. "Come on."

"But, you're givin` them time to make up a story."

"Not really. You'll see." I went around the side of the house, found a bush to stand behind near a window, and took out my cell phone.

"What are we doing? The windows are closed. We can't hear nothin`."

"Trust me," I said, turning on my phone voice recorder. "Go get that box."

201

"This is dumb," Zen said. "What are you doin` with that phone?"

"Shh, be patient. Go on now."

Puzzled, Zen ran. When she returned, she sat on the ground yoga-style with her elbows on the box. I continued to monitor my phone. We were about twenty feet away from Shorty and Mariana. When I heard the front door open, I powered it off. "Okay, let's go."

Zen unfolded herself from the ground, picked up the box, and followed me to the porch where Shorty was standing. "Where'd ya go?" he asked.

"Stretched our legs a bit," I said.

"Come back inside. We got somethin` to tell ya."

As I sat at the table, I reached down into my backpack and turned off my Bluetooth headset. Zen put the second box on the counter.

Mariana and Shorty sat on one side of the table. Zen and I on the other. Shorty had repositioned the chairs. Mariana's eyes were reddened. Shorty's expression was solemn.

"Mariana, you tell `em."

"It's my fault. I had no idea Tomas opened those statements. I've got a problem with spending too much. I was embarrassed. I didn't want Shorty to know. I knew he'd be mad at me." Shorty reached for her hand. "When Tomas went off to college, I changed my address to his. I told him I was doing it and asked him to not open my mail. He promised me he wouldn't." She broke into sobs. "He was always such a good boy, I never thought he'd go against his promise."

"And you were making the minimum payments?" I asked.

She nodded. "He was bringing my mail home once a month," she said, "and I took care of it."

"But then he stopped bringing the bills?" I said more to myself than to her. This was probably when Tomas began making larger payments to pay off his mom's debt.

She nodded again.

"And you didn't think that it was kind of odd that your statements had stopped coming?" Zen asked.

202

Mariana shuddered, interlocking her fingers and then releasing them only to do it again. "I know it's stupid now, but I had some notion that maybe my account got lost and the company was no longer billing me. I, ah, thought God had answered my prayers." She dropped her head on Shorty's shoulder.

Shorty put his arm around her and looked at me. "Do you think this debt has something to do with our son's murder?"

Mariana moaned.

"I don't know. It's possible. Anything is possible at this point."

I wasn't yet ready to question her about the ritual in the clearing.

38

"Are you telling me you bugged their house?"

"You never heard that from me."

Zen looked at me with suspicion written all over her face.

I smiled and took out my Bluetooth headset and iPhone from my pack. Placing them on my table, I switched on the recorder. Mariana and Shorty's voices came through loud and clear. I turned it off and looked at Zen. "You know nothing about this, okay?"

"Jessie! That's illegal. You could get thrown in the clinker. I can't believe you did that!" In the next second her look of horror transformed into an expression of amusement. "Whoa. Cool!"

I grinned.

"Do I get to hear it too?"

"Of course, we're partners in crime."

"Only when we're not being criminals. Where did you learn how to do that?"

"YouTube, of course. Where else?"

I switched on the recorder. We sat on the bed.

"She's still cryin`," Zen said.

I held up my hand for silence.

Mariana began to talk. "I didn't know he was workin` three jobs. I didn't know . . ."

"Okay, sit down. I'm listenin`," Shorty said.

"The money wasn't for me or us, it was for them."

"Them?" His voice reverberated.

"I've been helping our relatives back home. We're so lucky. We have a good life here. They have so little."

"Oh, Mariana . . . Mariana."

She caught a sob.

"Okay," he said, "tell me how you got involved."

"I've been . . . I've been going to Daniela Diaz for psychic readings. You know that. She told me she knew a way to get money over the border. I had to help. God wanted this. I know he did."

"You've been withdrawing cash from a charge card and giving it to that crazy woman? And our son has been trying to pay off your debt? Good God!"

Mariana sobbed louder.

"I know she got the money to them. She wouldn't lie to me."

"Oh sure she wouldn't. Have you ever heard from our cousins about getting any money?"

"No, but . . ." Mariana whimpered.

"It didn't occur to you that Tomas might have gone to this woman to get her to stop taking your money? If he did that . . . Mariana, did you ever tell Tomas what you were doing with all that money? It's not like you or our daughter have new clothes or we have anything fancy in this house."

"He never asked and I never said."

After this Shorty and Mariana discussed the lie they were going to tell us.

I turned off the recorder.

Zen shook her head. "That poor, vulnerable woman. She's been scammed."

"I wonder if all those people at the gathering were as well."

"Why couldn't she just mail the money?"

"She was probably convinced that it would be stolen long before it got to her relatives."

One thing I knew, there was a lot of money placed on that rock that night. I wondered how often the rituals took place.

So, what was Ty Chambers' connection with all this? Surely he was not helping aliens come to the states. How could I get him to talk? Then a twinkling Christmas bulb went off in my head. I looked at Zen and smiled.

"We need a break from all this—some distance to think about what to do next. Why don't you invite Ty Chambers to your place for a barbeque?"

"That jerky college dude?"

"Yeah, the one who seemed so interested in you."

"Ah, he was just being nice. He wouldn't come."

"Want to bet? I have his number."

Zen frowned. "What's the plan?"

"I'd like to get Ty here without him suspecting I want to talk to him and I'm thinking you might be the ticket for doing that."

"You want to *use* me?"

"Ah, come on. It's not like you have any interest in the guy."

Zen jutted her chin up. "I might."

"Ah, what could you possibly see in him that would interest you. He's a dweeb. You're a queen, besides you have Zebra."

"Not no more. He met a gazelle." Zen shot me a sideways glance, then broke out into a grin. "The jerk was kind of interested, wasn't he?"

"Oh, yeah."

"Give me that number."

Zen made the phone call. She hung up smiling.

"Told you," I said.

Zen looked like she'd swallowed a dollop of her favorite dessert, rich peanut butter pie.

"Oh, and Zen. I found several bags of cocaine in his room."

"He's a dealer?"

"Might be."

"Why that rat."

When Caitlin told Tomas who sold her the cocaine, Tomas must have confronted Ty. Ty was more than a rat. He was a murderer. But how to prove it?

On Friday night, Zen put on an ankle length skirt, a cotton blouse, and long hooped earrings. Her hair was loose. When Ty arrived he went right to her and presented her with a bottle of wine. Smiling, Zen put it on the picnic table. A fire burned in the firepot. I called out a greeting and lifted my bottle of Guinness.

Ty adjusted his look of disdain and tossed me a lopsided grin. "I didn't know this was a party," he said.

"I caught plenty of fish today. I like to pass on the abundance," she said, popping the wine cork. She picked up a ball jar and half-filled it, handing the glass to Ty.

"Aren't you having any?" he asked.

She reached for the bottle of beer on the table and tapped against his glass. "I'm a beer gal myself," she said.

He laughed.

Car doors slammed. I stood as Shorty and Marianna came into view. Mariana spotted Ty and froze. Ty swallowed the rest of his wine in one gulp, sending daggers to Zen. Zen gave him an "I'm as surprised as you" look.

Shorty looked from his wife to Ty then bent down to his wife. "What's wrong?"

She backed away.

"Mariana?" He took her arm and moved her away, standing under a coconut palm tree.

She spoke words we couldn't hear. He wrapped her in his arms.

Ty made a move to leave.

Zen stepped in front of him. "Where are you going? We haven't even had the fish yet." She put her hand on his arm and smiled sweetly.

He hesitated, then allowed her to lower him back to the table bench, talking non-stop.

In a rush of whispers Shorty came to me and confessed that Mariana had been giving money to the Diaz woman and her daughter to be used to help relatives in Mexico, emphasizing that Marian saw it as her Christian duty. Then, he turned to Mariana. "Tell her," he demanded, pointing at Ty.

She kept her head down. "He's been at several of the ceremonies."

Bingo.

I glanced toward Ty. Quickly, he looked away. Zen's hand was now on his thigh. "Okay, thanks for being honest, let's go talk to him."

"But . . ."

I interrupted Shorty. "You have to trust me. Come on."

"Mariana, come." Shorty pulled his wife forward.

Ty didn't look at us.

"Ty, you remember Tomas's dad, don't you? And this is his mother."

Ty stood and held out his hand. "Oh, of course. I thought you looked familiar. I'm sorry about Tomas. He was a stellar guy."

"As I'm sure you know they're deep in mourning and grasping at straws about anything and everything that could lead to the capture of their son's killer."

"Sure, my folks would do the same."

"At first, Mrs. Davis thought she recognized you, but she looked at you closer and decided she was wrong."

"I don't think we ever met except at the funeral," Ty mumbled.

"I just thought you'd want to know what all that drama was about that you witnessed. Anyway, I'll be right back. They came looking for me. I'll talk to them and be back in time for another Guinness. Party on, kids."

Zen and Ty smiled at each other. As we turned the corner I heard Ty laugh.

Good ole Zen, always there when you needed her.

After making Shorty promise that he would leave Ty up to me, they left. I rejoined Ty and Zen who weren't exactly kissing, well, not . . . well . . . whatever. When would that girl learn?

"Sorry for the interruption in the gaiety," I said. "Where were we?"

Zen jumped up and wrapped an apron around Ty's waist and announced he was the chef. He chuckled and took a plate of coated mullet from the outside fridge. Piece by piece, he laid a fillet on the hot grill. Zen hurried into the trailer and I sat on the bench watching him.

"Such a terrible shame to lose a son like that," I said, picking up my sketchpad and beginning to draw his likeness.

"Yeah. It can't be easy. Hand me that mitt, will you?"

"I heard some fool say: "At least there's one less wetback on the islands.""

Ty frowned. "I hope you set him straight. That kind of talk is hate talk."

"Oh, yeah. For sure." I smudged out a line.

"These immigration laws are ridiculous. We need to open the borders. Let people live where they want to live." He turned a fillet.

"I couldn't agree with you more."

He flipped two more fish.

Zen came outside and set a bowl of salad and a plate of sweet corn on the table. "Jessie is an artist. Did you know that?"

He raised his eyebrows in surprise. "Sure didn't."

"She has work in galleries here and in Fort Myers."

"Congrats. Two minutes and they're done," Ty said.

I put down my sketch and distributed the plates.

"America was founded on immigration," Ty said. "Where do people think all those New Englanders came from? Seed?"

Zen chuckled. "Yeah, maybe Injun's seed, that's where."

While Zen and Ty talked and shared jokes I mused about my problem.

I should call the sheriff and tell them everything I knew. Accept defeat. Let them get to the bottom of this. But the law

209

had been all but absent. Didn't look like Tomas's death had any priority at all. And I still had no proof.

"Jessie to earth. Jessie to earth. You still with us?"

I set down my fork. "Not really. I should go in. I need some rest." I stood. "Have fun kids."

Zen had given me her bed for the night. I pulled back the comforter and inspected the sheets before I climbed in. Not that I expected to see any bugs or anything.

The moon was high in the sky. Stars rained down in the distance. Inhaling the salt air, I gazed out the small high window. In my mind's eye I saw Will then Jay's face, each were smiling. I thought about Shorty and Mariana. How she had kept a secret from him and possibly doing that had cost their son's life, yet he still loved her. That was obvious. He would always love her—no matter what. He may not always like her, but he would always love her. I knew at that very moment that I would always love Will. My love for him was forever. Just because he died, my love didn't disappear—it just readjusted. Until I die, he would remain buried deep in my psyche. Our souls would meet again—somewhere. But I knew Will. He always wanted me to be happy. He would never want me to keep pining for him. Guilt closed too many doors—made you a half-person. Will would never want that for me. I'm no quitter. I'm a door opener. I gazed steadily at Jay's image until gradually the faces disappeared.

I opened my sketchpad and looked at my sketch of Ty. His shirt had an owl embossed above his shirt pocket—a tiny minuscule owl.

39

Later that night, having awakened with a start and unable to return to sleep, I turned on the tape recorder and listened to it several more times. Zen woke up and settled in a chair, watching and listening, saying little.

Switching off the recorder, I scrolled through the photos I'd taken at the clearing once again, reviewing my sketches and notes. Thinking. Looking for the thing I had missed. There had to be something. Some way to help me see how Ty Chambers fit into this puzzle. It was possible he was the murderer . . . that he ran a drug operation . . . that much of the money coming from the worshipers was given to him for cocaine. But I didn't think so. Why not?

I tapped my bare foot on the floor. Tomas had gone to Beadle first, then had gone to find his folks. Next he most likely phoned Caitlin. His dad wasn't home, but his mom was. Caitlin stopped at the Moores to get her great blue. Mariana Moore hadn't seen her do that. Where had Mariana been? The neighbors. Hadn't she said she'd gone to the neighbors? Daniela Diaz was Mariana's psychic adviser. Was it possible that Mariana had told her psychic that her son was frightened? Of what? Maybe she said she wasn't certain, but possibly it had to do with Caitlin.

Grabbing my cap and snatching up Gar, I headed out the door, Zen in tow.

We arrived at the Moore place at eleven p.m. The lights were on. I told Zen to hold tight.

Mariana answered my knock. She'd been crying. "Shorty's not here. He . . . he . . . left."

I stepped inside. "He'll be back," I assured her. "Come on, take a seat. I'm glad he's not here. I wanted to talk to you."

She looked at me quizzically.

"After Tomas left that night, did you stay home?"

"No, I told you, I went to Daniela's."

"That's right. Did you happen to mention to her that Tomas was upset?"

"Of course. We said a special prayer for him to Santa Muerta."

"Did you suggest why he might be frightened?"

"I said it might have something to do with Cat, but I wasn't sure."

Bingo.

"Have you spoken to Daniela today?"

She shook her head. "Her daughter said she'd left."

"The daughter is still at the house?"

"She said she was being picked up by a friend later tonight."

My heart skipped like a one-legged child—the friend just might be Ty Chambers.

I tried to keep the same expression. "Okay, thanks. Listen, get some sleep. I'll call you tomorrow. And don't worry about Shorty. He loves you. He'll be back."

I went outside.

Poor Mariana. I wondered how long it would take her to realize that she'd signed her own son's death certificate.

I opened the car door and slid in beside Zen. Pulling out my phone, I dialed 911 and reported a robbery at the Diaz's address. Backup was always a sound idea.

The Diaz trailer was dark. A white pickup was parked to the right. We slunk-walked to it and looked inside. Empty. We went toward the house.

212

No one answered my knock. I turned the doorknob and pushed the door open. Called out. Nothing. I reached for the light switch and flipped it. Nothing. No electricity. No boxes. No furniture.

We returned to my car, opened the glove compartment, and I pulled out my flashlight. "Let's go visit the chapel," I said.

The path was one of those winding things, but cleared. No-see-ums swarmed. We didn't stop to scratch. Instead, we hunkered down and continued on wishing we had eyes in the back of our heads.

The raspy sound of voices made us hit the ground. "Shh," I said, creeping forward.

The voices grew louder. One I heard. The other was soft and muffled.

"You think that redhead's not going to figure it out? Get real. She's no dummy." Youngish voice with accent. Sarah Peter's sister, Daniella's daughter? The other person's back was to us. Hooded sweatshirt. Gray sweat pants. Tennis shoes. It had to be Ty. If not him, who?

I bit my lip, burrowed into my pants pocket, took out my tape recorder, turned it on and laid it on the ground.

Again, the other voice was inaudible.

"Of course she will. But we'll be long gone. In a new place with new identities. Stop worrying. You want to end up like Sarah? May she rest in peace. Her mistake was that she told them she wanted out. Out? There is no "OUT" where the cartel is concerned. Keep your cool. They think you're losing it and you're dead meat. These guys are deadly. You knew that when you got involved with selling drugs on campus."

More murmurings.

"Shut your trap, you fool. My sister was dead the minute you killed Mariana's son. They knew she'd squeal. She was too attached to her students. You start whining and see where you end up. My mom starts yapping and I'll shoot her myself. All that dribble about helping people help their loved ones.

What a fool she is. She thinks I've sent the money to Mexico. Get real. Old people lose their logic.

Did you plant that coke? Good. I'll call the U tomorrow. That will take care of that stuck-up goody-two-shoes fool. Now, grab that money and let's get out of here. By tomorrow, we'll be on a plane to Costa Rica."

Heads down, they trotted our way.

I waited until the Diaz woman was level with my body, then slammed my leg across the path making a muscle-bound steel wall. She hit it hard and her knees buckled. Jettisoning up, Zen whirled and hit the other one across the left arm. A howl went up that would wake the ghosts of the dead. I raised my leg and for good measure, knocked the culprit out cold. The Diaz woman attempted to get up.

"Really? REALLY?" I said.

She glanced at my casts, at my long, muscular legs, at Zen, and plopped on the path of seashells.

"You have proof of nothing," she said, flipping her hair off her shoulder.

I took a step, bent down, picked up my recorder, turned it off and raised it over my head.

"Don't ever go to a party unprepared, my grandma always told me."

"Good God, look at this?" Zen was on her knees bent over the sweatshirt-clad body. I went to her side.

"You're kidding me!"

"Christ, didn't I tell you? Rich bitch."

Caitlin Howard moaned and moved ever so slightly. A great blue came out from under a tree, heading toward her. It stopped near her hand, bent and pecked her thumb. Caitlin's eyes opened. She saw the bird. Me. Zen. Half-smiling, she closed her eyes again.

Dammit, she'd hoodwinked me again. I'd got my man, it just wasn't the man I thought it would be; in fact it was a woman. Some days you just couldn't win for losing.

40

Jay walked into the room carrying a bottle of red wine and a bouquet of daisies. The door remained open to let in the cool breeze drifting over the pass.

"So the case is closed?"

"Yeah. Turns out the older Diaz woman was truly trying to help and Ty Chambers was actually sending money as well. He's like a major humanitarian. That was really hard for me to believe, but I reckon there are more outrageous things. The Diaz sisters and Caitlin were the ones deep into drug trafficking. Caitlin is singing like a mockingbird. She hid the cocaine under Ty's bed on a command of the Diaz woman. The feds are thrilled. They napped the captain. Seems he was tangled up in mangrove roots out on one of the outer islands. Been there for days. It'll be a while before he needs the service of a tanning studio. Seems someone took his clothes."

Jay cringed.

"Turns out Caitlin really did kill Tomas out of rage because he stood by her. Sad, huh?"

"Crazy sad."

"Why do you think Tomas didn't just give you some information about that weird skeleton doll?"

"I'm thinking he loved his mom too much to connect her to what was going on at the palm farm. He probably didn't fully understand what was going on himself. I reckon he left it up to me to see what I would find out."

Jay popped the wine cork. "The wonderful thing is that the drug ring in the area will be taken care of by the feds and all because of the actions of my ditzy redheaded artist friend, Jessie Murphy. People have already quit worrying and gone back to their island-time, peaceful lives."

"Hey! Don't call me ditzy."

"Zany then. I mean, come on, you hold conversations with a plaster of Paris garden-art gargoyle!"

My lips played with a smile. "Be careful, Gar is listening."

He chuckled.

A wok, a board filled with cut-up vegetables, a bottle of olive oil, and soy sauce sat on the counter. A cleaned and shelled bowl of fresh shrimp was in the refrigerator. The rice cooker had just switched over to "Warm." A plate of brie, crackers, and grapes had been set on the coffee table. The plate was surrounded by four burning white candles.

I sipped from my half-filled glass of wine. "Oh, and one more thing. Seems Caitlin's brother told his folks Caitlin wanted me to paint her portrait and they want to follow up with it. I told them it wasn't true, that Caitlin had no such desire, but they liked the idea. Guess I'll have some extra plane ticket money."

"Nice. Real nice."

"Absolutely."

"Couldn't have felt very good being outwitted by a younger woman."

"It didn't. But there you have it. When Caitlin told me her story, I felt sorry for her again and jumped to the conclusion she wasn't involved more than she said. I'm a sucker for a crying female."

Jay held out the flowers. "How are the arms?" he asked. "Better?"

I reached up, and careful not to bump his ears with my casts (now totally covered with signatures, caricatures, and various island flora and fauna) placed my hand on the back of his head and pulled him to me. Our kiss was long and yearning. When we pulled away, I said, "I missed you." And, oh, how I meant that.

He squeezed my shoulders and looked into my eyes. Like, I mean INTO. "You're not going to walk away from me?"

I shook my head. "I think my quick walking days just may be over."

His eyes twinkled. "Oh, sure. You'll quit your routine. I'll believe that when I see it."

"That's not what I meant and you know it." I stepped back and took his hand. "Let me," I said, unbuttoning his shirt. But after two buttons, the sound of a nearing boat engine made me hesitate.

The engine silenced. A grunt. Footfalls on dock. Muttering.

"Good enough. You'll like it here." It was Gator. Most likely alone, talking to his catch.

In the next second, two crabs scurried sideways past the open door, then disappeared over the side of the dock into the depths of the gurgling water.

"Have a good life." Gator said, raising his voice. "Hey, you two lovebirds, shut that damn door. I know you ain't decent."

Another grunt as Gator hopped into the boat. Then . . .

"Well, I hope they ain't decent anyways. Never can tell about young folk today. They can be awful damn thick," he muttered.

I smiled at Jay. He smiled at me.

ACKNOWLEDGMENTS

My gratitude to all who helped make this book possible.

Writers, critique partners, and editors: Marjorie Carlson Davis, Suzanne Kelsey, Claudia Bischoff, Jeannette Batko, Barbara Darling, Faith Gansheimer, Marsha Perlman, my Orcas Island bud, Sara Williams, and the Savvy Press gang for accepting me into their publication corral, especially Ellen Larson.

This book could not have found a more phenomenal cover artist than Peg Cullen or jacket designer than Carrie Spencer. To my editor, Betty Tyson, thank you is not enough.

During my journey, a New York author and editor, Lou Aronica inadvertently sent me on a learning path when he said, "You may not have the DNA to write a mystery." I thank him for providing that challenge.

To my family and my friends around the world. To those readers who continually asked when the second Jessie Murphy mystery would be out. To the more than gracious business owners and locals of Matlacha. To the crab fishermen of Pine Island I interviewed for another project I still plan to finalize: Thank you.

SNEAK PEEK

Prologue for the
Third Jessie Murphy Mystery

MAYHEM IN MATLACHA

"Hi baby girl, let me introduce myself. Don't know why I never done it before. Guess you make me feel shy. My mom tells me that since I dyed my hair I look like Lynette "Squeaky" Fromme of Charles Manson fame or a young Vincent Van Gogh who cut off his ear. That always makes me laugh. She might be partially right. I'm clever. Clever means you're like a fox, capable of sneaking up on someone without being detected. I inherited this trait from my dad. There wasn't nobody quieter, or sneakier than him, 'cept me of course. He used to say that he hated it that I had to be Top Dog in my classes. Well, I thought, but never dared to tell him, that's too damn bad, cause that's just what I am—Top Dog. I'm your biggest fan, soon to be your only fan."

The lithe form in the gloomy darkness took a step to the left, reached out and caressed a photo on the wall.

"I like your hair like that. It makes you look real sassy. But the cap, it's got to go. Makes you look like a man. And all that sleuthing crap. No way!

I know you're the type of woman who strives for perfection. I ain't seen anyone be more particular than you. Don't you get yourself in a stitch—our life will be perfect."

Taking four tacks out of the wall, an 8 x 10 black and white portrait of Jessie was removed. The stalker settled on the edge of the bed, stretched out and put the photo over a rapidly beating heart. A bouquet of flowers sat on the nightstand.

"Zinnias. Your favorite flower. My favorite flower. Best cut flower. Bar none. Reminds me of the one-acre patch we had growing outside my window when I was a kid. Fell asleep smiling at it. Woke up to it. But hell, when I was twelve I did something to piss off dad. Can't even remember what it was. Dad put on my favorite CD, took out his clippers and handed them to me. Took me until midnight to cut `em all down and dig up the roots. The mean sucker thought my sniveling was funny.

You know, you and me, we're going to have such fun. First, we'll drive to North Carolina. I know this town. We can rent a house cheap. We'll plow us up a garden plot, raise our own vegetables. Then what we'll do is become parents. Just one. Two is too much noise. I ain't good with noise. You and me will make real cool parents, nothing like mine or that bitchy grandma of yours."

The mattress squeaked with added weight.

"Of course, first I got to get you out of that stinkin` state of Florida. I hate palm trees and shark-infested water more than I hate plastic. And the painting? Sorry, woman, but that's a waste of time. Anyway, we'll be way too busy with the gardening, canning, and chickens—Oh, I forgot to tell you that—we'll have chickens too. Natural, organic, baby girl. That will be our goal. We won't need other people. We make our own little kingdom a couple of miles out of town."

Raising the stack of photos, intent, love-struck eyes gazed at the young woman in a bathing suit on a beach. She had just caught a volleyball and her head was thrown back as she laughed.

"There ain't nobody who'll ever love you more than me, Jessie. Nobody. We're soulmates. Destined to be together. Thinking of my life without you is the thing I hate most."

The mattress creaked again. Unlocking the nightstand drawer, long willowy fingers withdrew a bottle and a hypodermic syringe from a rusty, tin cookie box. The needle was adjusted and the right flannel shirtsleeve was pushed up. Intense, glittering eyes rested upon the strong forearm and wrist all dotted and scarred with puncture marks. With a solemn face, the sharp point was thrust home, the tiny piston pressed down.

ABOUT THE AUTHOR

jd daniels has a Doctor of Arts degree from Drake University with a dissertation of poetry. Her award-winning fiction, nonfiction, and poetry has appeared in various publications, including *The Light Between Us, The PEN Woman's Online Magazine, riverbabble, The Broad River Review, The Sylvan Echo, The Elkhorn Review,* and *Doorknobs & Bodypaint: An Anthology.*

She received a top award for poetry from Emerson College/Cambridge University in England. She is listed in the Iowa Arts and Poets & Writers Directories and is an active member of PEN Women of Southwest Florida, PEN America, Mystery Writers of America, and two writers' groups.

Coediting *Prairie Wolf Press Review* is another of her pleasures.

She cherishes being near the sea, traveling, and most of all laughing and talking with her friends and family. She continues to teach college-level writing.

Labelling herself an eclectic writer and a nomadic academic, she loves a challenge and follows her dream with passion.

See her website at www.live-from-jd.com

She'd love to hear from you.

OTHER BOOKS BY THE AUTHOR

FICTION

Minute of Darkness & Eighteen Flash Fiction Stories

NONFICTION

The Old Wolf Lady: A Biography
(First Edition)

The Old Wolf Lady: Wawewa Mepemoa
(Second Edition)

POETRY

Currents That Puncture: A Dissertation

Say Yes